THE GRAB

In Istanbul, a beautiful girl is grabbed from her hotel bed and taken out into the night. But Professional Trouble-Buster Joe P. Heggy is looking on and decides to investigate: who was the girl and why was she kidnapped? But when thugs try to eliminate him, he is equal to their attempts, especially when he's aided by a bunch of American construction workers. Then things get very tense when Heggy finds the girl — and then kidnaps her himself . . .

GORDON LANDSBOROUGH

♦

THE GRAB

Complete and Unabridged

LINFORD
Leicester

First published in Great Britain

First Linford Edition
published 2013

A catalogue record for this book is available
from the British Library.

ISBN 978–1–4448–1582–5

Published by
F. A. Thorpe (Publishing)
Anstey, Leicestershire

Set by Words & Graphics Ltd.
Anstey, Leicestershire
Printed and bound in Great Britain by
T. J. International Ltd., Padstow, Cornwall

This book is printed on acid-free paper

1

Kidnapped?

Some sound brought me from that body in the marble palace the Turks call a bathroom. And that was queer; for it wasn't much of a sound. Just something like a scuffle out in the alleyway alongside my hotel.

I don't know what there was about it, but it took me across to the long, high window, and as I went I threw that blunt, lethal instrument under the bed — my bed. I stood at the window and looked out.

First thing I saw was a cop. He was standing in the shadow cast by a high-riding silver-bright moon from the gloomy building across this narrow cobbled alley. But I could see him, and I didn't like him.

From that angle he looked squat, a round peg of a man with shining boot toes sticking out from under him. His face was blank, a thing of anonymity lost in the darkness under his peaked cap.

Yet I knew he was looking up at me, attracted by my sudden appearance at the window. It made me shiver, knowing I was being watched by a cop without a face — without a face that I could see, anyway. I'm a sensitive sort of guy, and I like my cops to have features. Then you can spot them in an identification parade, if ever you feel like asking for one.

Next moment I forgot about that cop. From right below some people spilled onto the alleyway. There were three of them. Two were men; the third — a girl.

They were big and round, well-fed and heavy-muscled, those men. They were wearing drape suits, American style, but I had a feeling right from the start they could never vote against Eisenhower — or Truman.

But it was the girl I looked at. Curiously, it's the girl I always look at. She was in pyjamas, and she was struggling in frantic fear against those apes.

2

A big car began to nose into view from a side alley. It was a large American sedan, and it was travelling without any lights.

The girl saw it and seemed to go crazy. She threw herself around, and I could hear her moaning, and then she got one hand free and tried to claw her way out of the grip of the other rube. But she hadn't the strength, and that egg seemed to be using his, making his grip hurt.

She was free for a fraction of a second only. Then the other rube grabbed again, and began to drag her towards the car.

I saw moonlight on her face right beneath me. She had jet-black hair, which said she wasn't a stranger to these parts, and her face was a terrified white oval. That light was so good I saw her eyes, and they looked like black pools pin-pointed with light — I saw her mouth wide open in a silent scream . . . yeah, a silent scream.

That gal was terrified, but for some reason she didn't dare let out a cry for help. I was to remember that later.

The buttons had snapped on her thin,

silk, pyjama jacket, and I had a momentary glimpse of a flat, white stomach and her breasts above it. Just a glimpse. Enough to encourage at a normal time, but this time was not normal. Not for Joe P. Heggy.

I went out of that room so fast I don't remember even opening the door. Maybe I went right through it.

For when I see a damsel in distress, I get kinda hot and wanting to do things about it.

You won't know Joe P. Heggy — me — of course, but let me tell you this. I'm just a corny sentimentalist at heart, for all the job I hold down, and the people I run around with. I'm chivalrous — yeah, chivalrous — where the fair sex is concerned. I'd give up my spare seat in my jalopy to any dame, blonde or brunette, any day.

Where dames are concerned, I'm soft, and that softness sent me leaping down the broad, shallow, marble steps, three flights down into the foyer.

The elevator? Sure they have an elevator in that hotel, but don't tell me

4

anyone ever uses the elevator in a Turkish hotel! Not at night, anyway. If it's not out of order, the old man who alone knows how to operate it won't be found, so you might as well use the steps every time. As I do.

There weren't many people in that palm-decorated foyer, but there was Benny behind the reception desk. Benny never seems to go home. Benny is the most important man in all Turkey, for he can speak American and he's nearly the only man in Turkish hotel service who can. He's a young man, who lived for many years in America and then came back to Turkey.

And he's slime, pure slime. An opportunist, if ever I've seen one. And I've seen plenty.

I shouted: 'What in hell's goin' on in the alley?' and that brought him to his feet, startled, his dark eyes seeming to jump all over his yellow face. He threw down his paper, but didn't come round the desk. Neither did he say anything. Even then I got the impression that he knew what was happening.

So I swore at him, because I was worked up, and I got the revolving door spinning and I ran round into the alley.

It was deserted. There was no one there at all. No cop. No apes with a struggling girl. And no car.

I stamped back into the foyer. Benny was trying to read. I stood across the desk from him and said: 'You can put that down, Benny. You're not seeing any words on that paper.'

Benny's face came out of the sheet, and he was scared.

Man, how that clerk was scared. But he kept his mouth shut. Benny normally likes to hear the sound of his Brooklyn-acquired accent, but this didn't seem to be one of the times.

I yapped: 'A couple of apes just dragged a girl out of this hotel in her pyjamas.' Benny said nothing. You'd have thought all the hotel's female guests left that way. 'She got thrown into a car and carried away.'

And Benny said nothing but kept looking over my shoulder, and he seemed a bit sick about something.

But he wasn't as sick as I was. Look, I'm not kidding, but my stomach was going round and round, remembering that silent struggle in the alley. It looked to have something to do with the police — maybe the political or secret police, if Turkey has such things. I wouldn't know. I don't know anything about the set-up in these countries, so far as police systems are concerned.

But I'm never quite happy in these countries when a cop's around. I always have a feeling of undemocratic influences — you know what I mean. Maybe I've read too many spy-thrillers, and swallowed Hollywood's idea of what goes in countries outside the Yew Ess Ay. Maybe.

But right then all I could see was a helpless girl, dragged into a car and taken off maybe to some secret-police prison somewhere. And I saw a lot of pictures flitting through my mind of what a bunch of flat-faced apes could do to a helpless girl behind walls where her moans wouldn't be heard.

Holy jeez, the thoughts I had in my mind were enough to set me jumping quicker than a bug on a hot griddle. I couldn't stand what I was thinking. I had to be a sap and try and do something about it.

I shouted: 'The hell, I won't stand for seein' girls treated thataway in any country. Not without standing on my hindlegs and mouthing a gripe agen it.'

I let my eyes drop to Benny's. I reckon I must have looked madder than mad, right then, and he was scared stiff of me.

He said, quickly: 'I got nothing to do with it, brother.' Always brother with Benny. He believed in democracy in some aspects. His quick, big dark eyes fluttered and looked away and then came back and then looked quickly away again. Benny was giving an impression of a man wholly out of ease with himself.

So I snarled something, and I kicked my way out through that revolving door, leaving Benny back of his desk under the yellow electric lights. I had an impression that he was reaching for the telephone, as I stomped away.

I went to the police station round the corner before I could cool off. I was in such a mood I was determined to make a song about the handling of that girl. I didn't care what she had done — if she had done anything.

Istanbul police are picked men. They all look six-footers, and they're physically first-class. But their uniform is something inspired by a Nazi stormtrooper's get-up, and we've been taught to dislike it in the Western World. So I wasn't on my best behaviour inside that police station. I was rude and arrogant, loud-mouthed and truculent.

I was scared.

Don't tell me most people aren't scared when they get inside the police stations of these countries around the Mediterranean. When you go in you have a feeling that maybe you aren't ever going to come out again. You feel anything can be done to you, and no one will be any the wiser.

Maybe we have read too much . . .

The main receiving room — or whatever it's called in these countries — wasn't sinister. It was small, not well-lighted, imposingly solid in its furniture, and comfortable looking.

Two big cops without helmets rose from a bench as I went in. Their eyes were upon me. They were tough babies, so I looked tough at them. A sergeant came in, buttoning his tunic. I don't know whether he was a sergeant, because I don't know Turkish police ranks, but I kept calling him that to myself and — well, take him as a sergeant and quit the sidetracking.

He spoke English, though not too confidently.

I gave him the story. 'I saw a girl taken from my hotel. She was in pyjamas. There was a cop standing by, watching the apes bring her out. He went off in the car with them, so it was police work.'

I took a deep breath. I always do when I tell a lie.

'I want to know what you're going to do to her. I want to see her. She's a friend of mine.'

That was sticking my neck out. It could bring a whole lot of trouble on me. But I was all worked up, I guess — sight of that partly dressed girl . . . had got me moving inside.

That sergeant just stared at me. He struggled with a foreign language and then said, blankly: 'No police have removed any girl from your hotel tonight.'

All right, what do you do under such circumstances? I did it, brother, I did a lot of desk-thumping, a lot of shouting, a lot of talk about seeing my ambassador. I even called them a lot of so-and-so's and generally behaved as an angry man, a bit scared of his surroundings, behaves.

But it did no good. That sergeant was impassively polite. He took all I had to give him and he just stared solemnly at me and repeated his statement: 'No police have taken any girl from your hotel tonight.'

Those other babies just stood around and said nothing and did nothing, and I think that scared me more than if they had behaved as truculently as I was. It gave me a feeling of utter helplessness. I felt that they must be sure of themselves to be able to watch my tantrums and listen to my yapping offensiveness, and be so stolidly silent all the while. It didn't occur to me until afterwards that

11

probably neither of them understood English, anyway.

Well, I got out of that police station after about five minutes. I knew I wasn't getting anywhere. I knew I could thump that desk until it was a ruin on the floor, and that sergeant wouldn't change his tune. I went out and I felt glad when I got outside into yet another of those narrow, cobbled, Turkish alleys which abound in Istanbul. There was the moon beautifully white and clear, riding in an absolutely cloudless sky. And the soft, warm, night air of summer along the Bosphorus was a joy to breathe after the claustrophobic atmosphere within that old police station.

I'm telling you all this, and I'm telling you what a so-and-so I am inside for all the big mouth I carry most times in my job. I felt the most relieved man on earth when I walked out on those cops.

I was also the most surprised man.

Somehow I hadn't thought it could be so easy, that I could go into a Turkish police station and shoot off my mouth and then swagger out, as I did. I suppose I'd been certain that there'd be a hellova rumpus, with a lot of shouted orders and heel clickings and the beginnings of an international situation. I felt for certain they'd try to slap me in the cooler and only release me when the American Embassy came down to protect an undeserving national.

Yet nothing like that happened. They just let me walk out.

I went along that busy main street of Pera, back to my hotel. That street is always busy. No one ever goes to bed before two o'clock in Istanbul. I moved along the crowded sidewalk, and this time I had no eye for the cuties who promenade by the hour along that fashionable shopping thoroughfare. And that shows the kind of emotion gripping me right then.

Usually I can think of nothing better than to amble slowly along that Istanbul sidewalk and gawk at the fashionable females who make this city such a Paradise for the traveller.

You see them of every Mediterranean nationality, from the dark-skinned Arabic types to the fair-haired Greeks who form such a large part of this population. And, brother, let me tell you those babies are sure good to look at. They seem to mature early and they have a softness and a roundness that somehow you don't seem to see back in the States or in more Northern countries. There's a kind of exotic touch about these females, something of the old Arabian Nights' magic, I suppose. They wear dainty, flimsy, highly-coloured dresses, and I'm telling you that any climate kind enough to keep women out of shapeless coats is a climate which suits Joe P. Heggy. There's a flamboyance about these Istanbul girls — a vividness — which somehow wouldn't go down in any other city in the world except perhaps Cairo.

But this night they could jiggle themselves past me and I never admired the goods, never even saw them.

I was still seeing that terrified white face in that alley. I was feeling the helplessness, the hopelessness, which had gripped that pyjama-clad girl, being dragged away by those shapeless, moon-faced apes.

I couldn't get my thoughts beyond that incident.

I went back into my hotel. Benny was behind his desk, and if he was reading that paper he'd got darned good eyesight. He didn't notice he'd got it upside down, and that shows the condition he was in at that moment.

I hesitated, looking at Benny, and it was at that moment that my brain began to come round to a significant little item — the girl could have screamed, but she hadn't done.

That was something to think about, because when a girl is terrified there's almost nothing in the world that will keep her voice free from the most ear-splitting screams. She had moaned, but had made no more noise than that.

I looked at Benny and I was thinking. 'She didn't want to go with them, but she didn't dare attract attention to herself.' And I couldn't make it out, couldn't understand it.

Benny looked at me uneasily over the top of his paper. He had crinkly black hair, and it was well greased, and under

15

that light it threw out highlights and made him look . . . cissyish.

I stopped looking at Benny because I didn't think it was going to do anyone any good. Instead I turned, intending to go up to see B.G.

Something timid quivered at my elbow and asked: 'Please, where can I get a guide book about the mosques in the old quarter?'

I took one look at her. That dame didn't rate for more than one look, and that not a lingering one. She wasn't my type.

She was English and you know what that means. Full of inhibitions, and ready to run away from what they would like to enjoy. And she was older than she should have been. Which means if she wasn't rising forty, she was trying to look more than her age.

But there's a heart of gold under the Heggy vest. I took time off to say: 'Ask that rube. He's got everything.' I looked coldly at Benny and added: 'And he knows a whole lot more than he makes out.'

Benny fidgeted and tried to smile but it made him look even more sick than usual. That boy sure had something on his mind right then!

I left that teetering middle-aged dame to get what she could out of Benny. I reckon her mind never rose higher than getting brochures out of any man, anyway. Which, maybe, is why she looked turned forty.

I went into the elevator, which again shows how distraught I was. After a couple of minutes I came out and climbed the stairs, and said vicious things with every stride I took. That old man who should have operated the elevator must have been having a session with a chambermaid somewhere,

I passed my room and thumped on the door next to mine. That's where B.G. was hibernating. And B.G., I might tell you, is my boss.

Strictly speaking, B.G. is the boss's son. The old man, back in Detroit, doesn't get around much now, because he'll never see seventy again. So he's put his little boy in circulation, and B.G. goes around the world where they have contracts and in general gums up the works.

He's what Europe fondly conceives to be a typical American businessman, and he knows it and tries to live up to the part. He's big and he's shaped like an egg and he's got about as much brain as an egg — one that's thirty days addled. He wears rimless, octagonal-edged glasses perched on a stub of a nose set into a big flat pancake of a face. And he's got a stomach that's no concern of anybody else except himself. In fact B.G. is mighty concerned about that stomach of his.

I forget now whether at that moment, standing outside his door, I was on his payroll or fired. He changes his mind so quickly. He won't get drunk and sometimes we do and then we get to forgetting that he's the boss and instead we think he's the sap he really is, and we treat him like that. He's got an unforgiving nature, and when we come out of the oil we generally find ourselves with a month's paycheck in our hand.

Yet somehow we always get back on the payroll.

This time we'd thought it funny to give B.G. a leg-up with his linguistic aspirations. B.G.'s the humourless, earnest, persevering type of man who tries to learn a few words of every language of the countries he visits. He trumpets that it makes the foreigner pleased to hear someone who's taken the trouble to learn at least a few words.

So we helped him. When he touched down at the airport he wanted to know what the Turkish equivalent was for 'Thank you.' We tried to help him.

After that he kept using the word and the Turks looked surprised but would politely take him and leave him outside the door in question. This happened about six times before he rumbled it. He didn't accept our explanation easily, either — that we'd made some awful mistake and instead of giving him the word for thank you we'd given the word which is seen mostly on that door where the ladies go in to powder their noses.

Call it rude humour if you like, but when the boys get together that's how they behave.

So we were all in the doghouse, and, as I say, I didn't even know whether I was on his payroll after that incident or available to look for another job.

I thumped on the door. To hell with B.G.; he's only the boss, anyway.

I heard the rattle of metal inside, and pricked up my ears. It sounded like — chains.

And then I heard B.G. call out to me: 'Who's there?' and I had a feeling he was in trouble even as he called out.

I shouted back: 'The hell, it's Heggy. What've you got in there — a dame at last?' And that was sarcasm, because B.G.'s got more inhibitions concerning the female sex than any man I've ever met.

He didn't rise to it this time, but his voice took on a note of quick concern, and he shouted: 'For God's sake, get the pass key and come in to me. My God, Heggy, I need you right now!'

So I found the floor servant with his tarbosh and I got him to open up. He wanted to come in and there was a big grin on that Turk's brown face, but I didn't see that it was any business of his, so I politely kept him out in the corridor.

I went into B.G.'s bedroom and B.G. was there.

He was lying on his back, spreadeagled, and fastened by wrists and ankles with shining chains to the four corner-posts of his bed.

2

The Police

I was so startled I had to sit down on the edge of his bed and smoke a Camel. I looked at him, the big slob.

He was wearing little trunks and a singlet such as athletes wear. Only, no athlete ever tried to shove a stomach as big as his into such a vest. He was without his glasses, but he could see me all right. Sometimes I used to think he didn't need glasses at all, but wore them to impress people. There was a lot of chicken around the heart of that big man.

B.G. got mad. That's what I wanted. I like to get him mad. It's a hobby of mine, getting bosses mad, and I'm expert at it and perhaps that's why I've had more bosses than most men.

He shouted for me to get him out of those things, but I just looked dumb and went on smoking.

I could see what it was. There were springs round those chains and it was one of these physical culture fads that grip men at times. That big stomach of B.G. had got him physical-culture conscious and it seemed I had discovered his secret. He did exercises to reduce it, here in his bedroom.

The idea was that you slipped your hands through a kind of handcuff, which was attached by springs and little chains round your bedposts. Your feet were thrust through similar footcuffs. And then you did exercises, like trying to sit up against the tension of those springs and trying to draw your knees up against the even more powerful springs, which fixed your ankles to those bedposts.

Me, I don't see any use in this sort of nonsense. Keep-fit is a pastime for adolescents. I stopped being an adolescent quite a few years back, and I just enjoy feeling out of condition. Maybe I'm not much out of condition, at that, and I don't have any bothers about a belly like the boss.

I looked at him coldly when he shouted

at me, and in time he got around to it that I didn't like being shouted at. So he became persuasive, and I like bosses better that way,

After a time I said: 'How do you get out of those things?'

He was exasperated but tried not to show it. He had also a confession to make and he didn't like making it and he mumbled over it. He was a man, in any event, feeling the indignity of his position. It seemed that you simply slid your hands through the cuffs but B.G. had thick wrists and big fleshy paws, and the exercising had caused them to swell and he couldn't get the cuffs over his hand. I felt inclined to leave the slob there, but that isn't the Heggy way. Joe P. Heggy is always a guy to give a man a hand in trouble, even if it is the boss.

Anyway, this was a good time to make profit out of the situation.

I said to him quite nicely: 'I don't know whether I can help you. I mean, I'm not working for you any longer, why should I dig you out of those damn bracelets?'

B.G. spoke earnestly. He said: 'Joe,

what are you talking about? Who says you're not working for me? You get this into your mind, Joe, that you'll always be working for me. Only, doggone it, dig me out of these bracelets, can't you!'

Well, that was good enough for me. I was still on the payroll. I dug him out. It took a lot of hair oil over his fat wrists, and he lost some of the skin in the process, but I didn't feel it, and I didn't smell like a nice boy afterwards.

He was ashamed of himself, as fat men always are ashamed when they've been caught out. I said: 'It's a good thing I came when I did.'

He stopped washing himself under a tap labelled: 'Chaud' but it wasn't. Like the elevator, the hot water system never worked in this hotel, either. He looked at me and said, suspiciously: 'What did you want of me at this time of night, anyway?'

I said: 'If anything happens to me, B.G., I want you to remember what I'm telling you now.'

I saw that big, flat pancake face come round quickly, apprehensively, the electric light reflecting greasily upon his feature-less face. That B.G. got in a panic quicker than any man I've ever known, and him with all his millions.

'What d'you mean, Joe? Don't tell me you've got into more trouble?'

Now, that's good, coming from the man who employs me. Back in the States my job was trouble-buster. If there was trouble anywhere within the Gissenheim empire, I was the boy who was sent down to eliminate it. You know what sort of trouble you can get — rival firms sabotaging your supply trucks; trouble among two-timing salesmen who are selling out to rivals; and some labour disputes, though I don't like them. I even had to go and take part in a revolution once, in the Central Americas, when a lot of Gissenheim property was at stake.

Well, here I'm employed as a trouble-buster, and the man who employs me suddenly turns round and asks sharply if I've been getting into trouble! I shut him up with a flip of my paw. You could always shut up that big fat slob if you knew how to flip confidently and contemptuously enough. You should try it on the boss someday. You'll probably be surprised at the result.

I said: 'Listen.' And then I told him what I had seen out in the alley, and then what had happened down at the police station — though, come to think of it, just nothing had happened there.

'But I want you to know this, B.G. — there's something very deep and very nasty afoot, and I've got myself mixed up in it.' I lifted my hand when I saw his fat mush splitting to make some heavy statement. 'And you can forget what you were just about to say. Any time I see a girl in trouble like that, I feel I've just got to jump in with both feet.'

'But now you're in with both feet — ?'

'Things might happen to me.' I brooded over my Camel. I'd got a hunch that things were going to happen to me, and B.G. was something in the nature of an insurance policy. I looked at him. He was scared. He didn't like foreign parts, because he was far out of his depth in dealing with people beyond his own family circle. That's how I always looked at it, anyway.

'I've got a hunch that I might get slung into a sedan like that dame. Okay, B.G., if you don't see me around for a while, you go down to the American Embassy and bellyache to high heaven about me. Get the dragnet out and find me. I'll be somewhere around, though my guess is I won't be wanting to be where I am.'

That was a good sentence, and it made B.G. think a bit. It made me think a bit, too. I didn't want to be where I didn't want to be. B.G. wasn't much of an insurance policy, but I couldn't think of anything better to do right then. I tell you, I'm a timid kind of guy, always running away from trouble. But I can take care of myself if trouble comes running after me.

B.G. put his glasses on, as if that helped him to think better. His thinking didn't seem to do him any good because he finally took them off and went in for a shower without saying so much as a word to me. Perhaps he would have liked to have made cutting comments, but he must have been remembering the undignified position I'd found him in a few moments ago. And he knew by now that Joe P. Heggy could hold his own when it came to making cutting remarks.

He closed the door of his bathroom, and locked it. That's the kind of sap B.G. is. He doesn't like to be seen, not even by his own sex, when he's in the nude. I don't go that way myself at all, but that's the way some men are built, I guess.

So I shouted through the keyhole. 'Hey, are you plannin' to go out?'

Because one of my jobs was to keep the boss's son out of trouble. He was such a sap that his father knew he needed a nursemaid, and so he'd picked on me.

B.G. yelped back: 'I think I'll go to the *Gazino* for supper.'

I shrugged. That meant I had to go, too. So I went back to my room to get changed. Anyway, there was nothing for me to hang around this hotel for, and the *Gazino* was a pleasant place for supper, anyway.

It was only when my hand was feeling for the door key that I remembered that body in the bathroom. I felt sick inside. I just naturally hated what I'd just done.

But there was nothing else for it. I had to go in and face it.

And then I found I had no key.

And then I found Benny standing by my side and he had a key in his hand. Benny had anticipated this moment and had come up the stairs or the elevator to help me in distress.

He spoke quickly. 'I guessed you'd have locked yourself out.' My key was inside my room. He was a good guesser.

I took the key and looked hard at Benny. I thought: 'You slimy so-and-so, you're trying to get around me, aren't you?'

But I didn't say anything aloud to Benny; I just let him read what I was thinking in my face. Benny mustn't have liked what he read there, and he quit trying to be nice. He went away, and I heard him say something that sounded suspiciously like: 'The hell, you can get yourself out of trouble in future.'

I didn't beef after him. I don't give a damn if hotel servants do stand on a level with their patrons. After all, aren't we supposed to be democratic?

I went into my apartment. I turned to go into the bathroom, because there was something I had to get over. I'd got to dispose of that body.

There was something moving on the floor, just inside. I reckon it was its mate. It was about four inches long, and brick red, and it ran around in quick frantic circles when I switched the light on. A kind of cockroach, you'd say, only the granddaddy of all cockroaches if it was. Anyway, I don't know if cockroaches ever go brick red, as these Turkish crawlers do. I jumped on it. That made two bodies to dispose of. And, boy, how my stomach turned as I felt my heel go crashing through that shelly body. That's the worst of some of these Middle East hotels. You've got to share your room with things which shouldn't be there.

I scooped up the remains and put them in the marble pan which had been made in Victoria's time by some firm at Gateshead, England. Then I flushed them away.

I'd just finished my shower and was climbing into my natty white suiting, when there was a polite tap on the door.

I went across, fastening my shirt. When I opened the door I saw the corridor was filled with uniforms.

That's how it looked to me, anyway. There was a big guy, some sort of officer I guessed, in the Istanbul police. He was built on mighty lines, though young. A really powerful man, smooth-shaven, red-faced, rather good-looking, but tough, boy. Mighty tough.

Back of him I saw several other cops. Maybe there were only two or three, but right then my mind kind of exaggerated everything. That corridor looked lousy with police.

I said, firmly: 'I don't want to buy anything,' and tried to shut the door.

One of the cops had his foot against it, and it didn't move. So I looked sourly at that big, young officer and said: 'I've got my passport. It's in order. The best in the world. American.' I wanted him to know what he was up against if he was looking for trouble . . . Uncle Sam.

For I was expecting trouble. I'd got this hunch in my mind that trouble was going to come dropping down on me because I'd seen something I wasn't supposed to see . . . and kicked up a fuss about it afterwards. Now it looked as though that hunch was correct. Cops don't fill a corridor for nothing.

He gave a little deprecating wave of his gloved hand, and said: 'I'm quite sure your passport is in order, Mr. Heggy.' He said it politely, too, and that added to the surprises of the night.

He spoke with an American accent that was assured and told of residence in the States rather than tuition in our language at the American College along the Bosphorus. Clearly he had received his education in America.

I looked at him suspiciously, all the same. I just didn't trust these monkeys at all.

He went on to say, still so politely: 'Your visit to the police station was reported to me. I thought that I would like to speak to you on the subject personally, Mr. Heggy. Please accept my apologies, but your statements, you see, do demand police investigation.'

I said: 'The hell, what is there for you to investigate?' That girl, I was still sure, had been whipped away by Turkish police, and I wasn't to be kidded by this big, well-spoken, calm-looking young man.

But he was shaking his head. 'Mr. Heggy,' he said, and his voice was very firm, 'we can't allow girls to be abducted forcibly from hotels in this city. You may have imagined what you say you saw — '

'Brother, I never imagined what I saw,' I rapped with equal firmness.

'Then you see, Mr. Heggy, we've got to enquire into these statements you have made.'

He was so calm, so polite, but so firm with it. I kept looking at him, trying to read what was behind that big brown-red healthy face of this young police officer. And my eyes sometimes flickered beyond him, to those monkeys of his in the passage. They were all such big men, filling their uniforms with solid muscle, and I couldn't help feeling that if it came to a shindig I was going to get the worst of it.

And Joe P. Heggy just naturally hates to get the worst of any fight.

The officer said: 'Perhaps you would like to discuss this matter further inside your room, Mr. Heggy.' He looked significantly down the corridor, where a few guests, heading for the elevator or stairs, were caught in that irresolute pose of people wanting to do two things at once — and one of them was to gawk at a man in trouble with the police.

I thought there wasn't anything else I could do about it. I had a feeling that if I said: 'No, to hell with it, you stay out in the corridor,' these monkeys would just force their way into my room.

I stood by grudgingly, and I felt like giving them Lincoln's Address at Gettysburg. I was fully determined to kick up the goddamnedest row ever heard in Istanbul if they tried any police tricks on me.

Brother, I was in for yet another surprise! The police officer stepped into my apartment, and closed the door after him upon his men.

I said rather suspiciously: 'Don't you want your strong-arm boys in with you?'

He laughed and took off his gloves. I had a feeling he was laughing at me. He said, tolerantly: 'No, Mr. Heggy, I don't think we need any witnesses to our conversation. This is a friendly call, as I'm sure you'll appreciate, and I'm out to help you.'

Suspiciously — 'Help me? Now why in hell's name should I need helping?'

His eyes widened in surprise, and yet I was sure he was mocking me. He said: 'But you told them at the station that this girl who was carried away was a friend of yours?'

I swallowed. That comes of telling lies. One was coming home to me now. I thought George Washington had something, right then, and I made a lot of vows for the future. One of them was to keep my big nose out of other people's affairs.

The officer said, patiently: 'Now, Mr. Heggy, will you please tell me in your own words exactly what you saw? Please tell me absolutely everything, and don't omit any detail.'

I found myself telling him the tale. I started by thinking it was a waste of breath, that this guy must have known the full story better than I, but I ended up feeling entirely different.

He knew I had changed towards him, because when I had finished, he said, quietly: 'This has nothing to do with the police. I think now you are believing me, aren't you, Mr. Heggy?'

I was grouchy in my admission of the rightness of his statement. The hell, a man doesn't like to admit he's been a bit of a fool. It made me feel like some kid stuffed with fantastic novelettish or filmic notions. But I was convinced, and Joe P. Heggy at times can do the big thing.

I growled: 'Yeah, I've got to change my mind I reckon.' I changed it so much I went over to a sideboard and dug out a bottle of best Scotch. I said: 'I'll make amends with a drop of good liquor.'

The young police officer laughed. He said: 'That's unnecessary, Mr. Heggy. We're rather used to other nationals getting curious ideas about our police forces.' He shrugged. 'You've got to remember, though, that we're not an advanced country such as your own.'

He didn't continue, and maybe he was wise, because there was no sense in taking up time arguing about degrees of democracy — or totalitarianism.

Instead he said: 'What you have told us sounds very serious. We've got to find out who has kidnapped this girl. You think she was Turkish?'

I nodded. 'Could be. Or maybe a Bulgarian or from one of the adjacent countries.'

He smiled. 'That,' he said dryly, 'won't help us very much. I want you to give me your description of this girl.'

I said: 'Look, brother, why don't you go down to Reception and ask that two-timing Benny something about his female guests in this hotel? He should know who's in the hotel, and he should be able to say who's missing now.'

That young officer was watching me all the time I spoke. There was a thoughtful look in his calm, rather humorous-looking brown eyes. Then he said: 'I've already spoken to the night receptionist.'

'Yeah?'

'The man you call Benny says he has been round the hotel and can account for all the female guests.'

We looked at each other for a few seconds. And then I took a deep breath and I came out heavily with: 'Benny's in on this, whatever it is. He's a slimy sonovabitch, and money will get him to do anything or say anything.'

I looked at the police officer to see what he thought about my statement. But he was a police officer, and trained to be diplomatic. He merely nodded, and that could mean anything.

I was raw inside about Benny's statement, because it clashed with my own. In fact it made my story sound like the hotted up imagination of an incipient D.T. And I hadn't been drinking, so far this evening.

I started in to say: 'Look, that girl was wearing pyjamas. Leastways, some of the pyjamas was still on her.' I was thinking of that glimpse of firm, rounded young breasts when the buttons came off her jacket in the struggle. 'That girl must have been staying in this hotel to be dragged out in her pyjamas like that.'

But even as I said that I saw the fallacy of the argument. Or at least I saw a possible explanation of it all, and I reckon that young officer saw it, too, but he didn't say anything.

It won't be the first time that a husband and friends have surprised an unfaithful wife with some ardent lover in an hotel apartment. Maybe this was just such a case. Maybe those big, heavy-muscled men had been dragging home a naughty little wife.

Maybe.

But I didn't think so. It just stuck in my craw, that theory. I mean, when things like that happen they're not planned to include a cop standing guard to cover the proceedings — and a bribe sufficient to keep a man like Benny lying to the police.

I didn't feel she was any erring wife. I felt there was something infinitely more sinister behind this carefully laid scheme to snatch a girl out of her bedroom at night.

The young officer was very serious. He said: 'The important part of your statement, so far as we are concerned, Mr. Heggy, is that you insist that one of our policemen was complicit in this affair. Now that's a most serious statement to make.'

I said: 'Serious? Well, brother, I repeat it. There was a cop in on this snatch.'

I heard the officer murmur: 'I believe you, Mr. Heggy. Or at any rate, I believe that someone masqueraded as a policeman to help in this abduction'

You know, at that I breathed a tremendous sigh of relief. I'd just got around to believing this cop when he said that the Istanbul police had nothing to do with that kidnapping, and now I was mighty glad to realize that this big officer believed my story. I mean, without any other witness, I had to admit that my story sounded thin. Okay, to have it believed, was quite a touch of flattery to the old Joe P. Heggy ego.

He was looking thoughtfully at his big

smooth hands — hands that hadn't done much manual labour in their time. They were strong and well-cared for. Then his eyes lifted to mine and he said, very thoughtfully: 'We don't allow people to masquerade as police. We're going to find out who these people are.'

I said, heartily: 'Good for you, brother. And at the same time find that gal.' I was also thinking, 'And when you do, introduce me to her.' For she was quite a dish, that jane. And I'd seen more of her than most men, I suppose.

The big young officer threw back his head and laughed, and for some reason it wasn't a reassuring sound, though there was plenty of humour in it. So I looked at him, suspiciously, and growled: 'Who's the big laugh for, brother?'

He was on his feet, pulling on his gloves. He looked at me, his brown eyes twinkling, and he said, so casually: '*You'll* find them for us, unless I'm mistaken.'

I looked at him. And then I went for another Scotch. I said, sourly: 'What do you mean?'

But I thought I knew what he meant,

42

because I figured that he'd got the same sort of mind as I had. In other words, he was figuring that these boys might soon take a crack at me.

He confirmed my theory by saying: 'They seem a desperate lot of people, whoever they are, Mr. Heggy. I mean, there must be something pretty big behind it all for men to do a thing as daring as that — even to posing as a police officer. So, my guess is that when they hear you were a witness to their activities, they might try to eliminate you.' He seemed to pick that word eliminate, carefully, as if he wished to be tactful on an unpleasant subject

I knocked back that Scotch and then I said: 'Let 'em all come, brother. They'll find Joe P. Heggy waiting.'

I reckon that alcohol had something to do with my bravado, because I'm telling you I'm a nervous, sensitive man.

The cop officer went out at that, and I was surprised to see that corridor empty, as if his monkeys had gone off to do some other work. He saw my questioning look, and said with a smile: 'They're checking on the clerk's statement. They'll be going to every room and questioning the people there.'

I thought of B.G., and his palpitations when a Turkish policeman began to question him. It did me good to think of the fat slob palpitating, and I felt pleased for the first time about this affair in consequence.

The cop went, and I realized that almost for the first time in his life, Joe P. Heggy was a friend of a policeman.

I went back and finished my dressing. Then B.G. came barging in. He doesn't knock, ever; he figures a boss has a right to walk in on a man even though he'd gripe if anyone did that to him. So I figured I could tell him what I thought of his manners and I did. And then I thought I'd put a scare on him.

I said: 'B.G., I'm a marked man. If you go with me, you run the risk of stopping a knife or some lead intended for Joe P. Heggy.'

I watched his big, fat, pancake face while I said this, and I enjoyed the quavering fear that came up from his chicken heart at my statement.

I said, hopefully: 'Of course, you can always go out by yourself.'

I didn't like playing Nurse Nelly to this egghead, and I'd been looking for a way of ditching him so that I could enjoy my own company without thinking all the time of his inhibitions.

But B.G. didn't take the offer. He was dead scared of going out alone after dark in a foreign city. I reckon he was stuffed even fuller than I was with tales of thuggery in those primitive parts of the world outside law-abiding Detroit. He was torn between the devil and the deep blue sea, but the devil won, as he always does, in the end.

He said: 'I think you're exaggerating. It doesn't matter, anyway — you're coming with me.'

That was why I had been employed by the old man — to take care of little Berny Gissenheim on his travels abroad.

It made me sourer than usual, because I was in no mood to enjoy the boss's company. I wanted to think, and if I couldn't get a solution to my thoughts I wanted to get drunk with the boys, and all that was denied me if I was with B.G.

But — he made out the paychecks. What he said had to be. So we went out together and down the stairs because there was a notice on the elevator: 'Out of Order'. It was written in three languages to make sure. My guess is that notice went up every time the old man who ran the elevator had a date with one of the chambermaids.

Down in the foyer Benny got agitated so much that he began to work when he saw me. Anyway he went through the motions of doing a lot of writing in a big ledger. There was a guy sitting on a bench to one side — a hard bench reserved for visitors calling upon guests at the hotel — probably hard in the hope of making their visits infrequent. He was reading a newspaper and I remembered thinking at the time that that newspaper must be mighty interesting to keep a man up hear midnight reading it on a hard bench.

I was going across to make Benny feel really uncomfortable when something timid touched my elbow.

Something timid said: 'He didn't have any. He says he's run out.'

I looked down. There must be something reassuring about the Heggy physiognomy after all for timid dames twice in one evening to pour out their little troubles to me.

I looked meanly at Benny and said: 'You don't want to believe that guy. Lady, he's holding out on you, I tell you.'

That would be just like Benny, I thought. Benny would take it out of a timid dame like this fluttery female just because he lost out in an encounter with Joe P. Heggy.

She looked wistfully at the pigeon-holes behind Benny's bowed head where he worked at a table behind the desk. Benny, I knew well enough by this time, was trying hard to avoid the Heggy eye.

I heard her say: 'I would have loved to have seen those mosques in the moon-light.'

Next second I heard B.G.'s big mouth yapping. He wanted to show off, I suppose, and this timid little dame must have made him feel big and good.

He said: 'That's no place for a lady after dark. You should keep away from such places because you never know what sort of characters are waiting around for the innocent tourist.'

That little dame turned on him, all fluttering and pink and her eyes hardly daring to lift to his face. It's routine No. 1 with most dames, but I reckon that B.G. isn't worldly wise. She kept saying: 'Oh, thank you for warning me. It's very good of you. I hadn't realized that it might be dangerous.' And then a lot more eye fluttering and then she said: 'That's the disadvantage of being a frail woman instead of a big strong man.'

She did everything except say: ' . . . Like you,' but that would have spoilt things — it would have overdone it, if you see what I mean. And I, standing there nodding my head cynically, saw the fish take the bait and the hook and the line and everything.

It made him feel big and strong and good, and I could see the air go into his chest and fill it out, and I knew he was holding that fat-gut of his so that he looked muscular instead of beefy. He was looking at her tolerantly, in a strongman manner, through his impressive-looking American businessman's glasses, and he was saying: 'Perhaps I might find the time to escort you around the mosques, if you're staying at this hotel.'

She started fluttering again and thanking him and putting in the odd sentence, which made him feel pleased with himself. I had to hand it to the old gal. She may have been doing it unconsciously, but she had the right line of patter to please B.G.

I even looked at her suspiciously, because she never struck a false note. And yet she was innocent. She was just a timid middle-aged dear saying the right things because she had been brought up to say them, and she couldn't think differently.

I also thought that she looked better than when I'd first seen her. Her face was pinker, and it seemed to give her a little — shall we call it, bloom of youth? And when I looked down her trim neatly-dressed little figure I thought that maybe the gal wasn't in too bad shape after all.

That's something I've noticed before. Every woman has some pretension to beauty. It's queer, but the first time you see some women you don't think anything about them at all. Then, when you've seen them a few times, you begin to wonder how you missed those little feminine things which make them attractive to we wolves of the world. Some women kind of grow on you. Like oysters and a lot of other things, I suppose.

I turned. I wanted to speak to Benny. And as I turned I let my eyes trail on the big boob who was my boss.

He was simpering. You tell me if there's anything more sickly than the sight of a big fat sham-businessman simpering!

He was making small play with his glasses. You know what I mean, taking them off and polishing them and then sticking them back on his stubby little wart of a nose. He was still holding his stomach in, and by now it must have been hurting a lot, because there was a lot of stomach and he hadn't held it in for years.

Before him, eyes modestly downcast,

was that small, rather dainty, rather dowdy piece of goods from England. It was queer to think that that passed-over portion of feminine frumpery could arouse anything in the male breast. Honest to God, not in ten thousand years, could she have quickened my pulse by so much as one extra heartbeat.

And yet in some way she appealed to B.G. I suppose at heart he knew he was a sap and that most men regarded him as such — and most women, too. And I suppose he was wanting a bit of flattery from the other sex, just as we all do. Now he was getting it, and he didn't seem to see the old-maidishness of his flatterer.

I let my eyes trail contempt across his face, letting him see my cynical amusement. It made him blush and become indignant and he switched off that sickening expression of simpering coyness. I never miss a chance to make a boss feel uncomfortable. Why the heck should I do otherwise? Don't they make me feel uncomfortable all the time?

I left them. There was a whole lot more important things on my mind than B.G.

and the old maid.

Benny saw me coming and pretended he didn't. He was making out bills, I suppose, and doing a lot of frowning, as if he was mightily preoccupied.

I leaned on the reception desk, and never said a word but just stared at him. After a time he had to drop his pose, and then he looked up at me and with the fear in his brown, shifty eyes, was anger. At that moment I knew that if there was anything mean and nasty that could be done to Joe P. Heggy, Benny would clamour for the job.

3

Surprise!

I said: 'Benny, I want the hotel register.'

He got up, shuffling some papers angrily between his hands. But he had the sense not to let the anger show too openly on his face. He said, sullenly: 'You're not allowed to see the hotel register.'

I looked surprised. I even held my hands open appealingly towards him. 'You can't be right, Benny,' I said soothingly. 'Every guest must sign the register in this country.'

He rapped back: 'But you've already signed it, Mister Heggy.' And I knew he was on the run or he wouldn't have given me the mister. That boy had lived in God's Own Country, and he liked to demonstrate his ideas on equality and democracy with his guests. Mister, in fact, was quite an achievement.

'Maybe I didn't fill in my particulars

exactly,' I said. 'Now, Benny, you wouldn't want me to get into trouble with the police through putting down wrong particulars, would you?'

He knew I was sassing him. And I knew that he'd love to get me into trouble with the cops. But he didn't have any real excuse for holding out on me, so, grudgingly, he brought out the dilapidated book which was the hotel register. I took a good five minutes over the job. I checked through every room number allocated to a guest, and in the end I was able to look up at Benny and say: 'You've only two female guests staying alone in this hotel, haven't you?'

I'd worked it out in my mind that the girl who had been snatched must be on her own. Otherwise, if she had a husband, or even a girlfriend staying with her, there'd have been a ruckus following the abduction.

So it seemed to me the thing was to find out how many unaccompanied women there were in this hotel.

There were two. I looked at the names. The first was Lavinia Dunkley.

Nationality British. Last address, London, England. The other was Marie Konti. Her nationality was given as Turkish.

I lifted an eyebrow towards Benny. He wasn't worth more than that. I said: 'Lavinia Dunkley?'

He nodded sourly beyond me, to where B.G. was being made to feel a man by that wisp of neglected womanhood. So that was Lavinia. The name seemed to fit.

I said: 'Marie Konti?'

This time he was doing things with a very heavy ring on his finger. I always watch a man's feet and hands when I'm asking questions and I'm going to doubt the answer. When a man — or a woman, for that matter — makes bargains with the truth, they often show it by a little incautious movement of their limbs. You watch out for it, next time you're suspicious, and see what I mean.

Benny was fiddling rather quickly with that ring as he answered, and I had a feeling that he didn't want to discuss Marie Konti. He said: 'She's upstairs.' And then he put acid into his mouth. He said, nastily: 'The police have been before you, Big Boy.' That was a return of his old arrogance. Benny was the kind to try to get his own back.

I wasn't taking his word for anything, so I made a note of her room number. It was 102 and that was on a floor above my own.

On an impulse I thought I'd drop in and see Marie Konti. That is, I'd see her if she was there. Because my theory was that Marie Konti might be the girl who had been dragged away in the night by those apes. I had a feeling she wouldn't be in her room.

That feeling grew as I mounted the four flights of steps — the elevator man wasn't around again. I thought maybe I'd better start looking closer at the chambermaids to see what there was in them which put them above duty.

I came out on to the fourth-floor landing — an impressive balustraded area with a passageway, which led between the closed doors of silent rooms on either side. I walked down the thick Turkish carpet, under soft-glowing lights, which surged in intensity with fluctuations of current from the overburdened Turkish power stations. I came to room 102.

I knocked. No one came to the door.

I knew no one would.

I knocked again, louder. And I was thinking: 'So it was Marie Konti who was snatched.' And I was wondering who Marie Konti was and why she had to be snatched.

And I wondered why it was, even in her terror, she hadn't dared to scream.

I lifted my hand a third time to knock, and then the door opened and Marie Konti was standing there before me.

I was so startled for a moment I could only stand and look at her. Let me describe her.

She was a swell-looker. That's for a start. She was rather tall, and rather slim and very dark, though I don't think she was Turkish originally. Maybe Hungarian. Maybe Roumanian. Maybe Italian. I never can tell the difference.

She had good hair and it was glossy black and fell in long waves, as if she had been combing it and had just thrown it back over her shoulders. She had a rather long, thin face, but attractively so. Her eyebrows were unfashionably thick, but they gave her face character far beyond that of any pencil aid. She had rich, ripe lips, though here she had applied rather too much lipstick. Her eyes didn't match her appearance. That was why I thought she wasn't Turkish. Her eyes weren't brown, which you'd expect from a Turk, but were grey and slumberous. That is, her eyelids seemed to droop a little over them, and whether that was a natural way with them, or whether it was a pose designed to protect her eyes from being too easily read, I don't know.

She was dressed in one of those bright, beflowered dresses which look just right in this rather exotic climate and yet would be garish in more northern climes. It fitted her and it showed up her figure and — wow, what a figure!

That girl had everything and that dress let you see it, almost.

She looked at me and said: 'Yes?' And I knew I had been recognized immediately for what I was — an American.

At that I gulped, and the old Heggy brain began to work again. I said: 'I — er, I'm looking for Miss Marie Konti.'

She said, still in the same questioning voice: 'Yes?'

So I said straight out: 'Are you Marie Konti?'

She nodded. 'But of course.'

Then we both stood and looked at each other for a second, and I could have gone on looking at her, because she'd been made for that purpose. She was looking at me, too, and I don't think there's much about the Heggy frame to get a girl antagonistic. Anyway, in these countries the local girls don't look at the man; they fall in love with the accent. The American accent speaks of dollars, and the world's hungry for our greenbacks.

I was climbing out of my surprise pretty quickly, but curiously I was not climbing out of my suspicions.

For some reason I looked at that girl and thought: 'You're not Marie Konti. You can go on telling me you're Marie Konti until your face is royal purple, but I won't believe it.'

Maybe I was obstinate. Maybe I just didn't want to feel I'd made a fool mistake. I looked coldly at that dame and let my eyes tell her what was in my mind. I'm polite, where ladies are concerned, and don't generally tell them when I think they're lying. I had a little impression of her eyes flickering past me, and I turned at once to see what was creeping up behind. There was nothing.

That corridor was empty save for myself. All the doors along the corridor appeared to be shut closely. I told myself I was getting unnecessarily jumpy, and switched my eyes back to that attractive girl in the doorway. And that attractive girl suddenly decided to invite me in.

She smiled, and she had good teeth. Her eyes weren't slumberous any longer. They were bold and inviting, and when I saw them, I thought: 'This gal's been around a bit.' She knew how to handle men.

I went in. I don't remember the last time I refused an invitation from an attractive girl to go into her apartment. Anyway, there was a lot I wanted to know about this girl who said she was Marie Konti.

I closed the door behind me and then took a little precaution . . . The girl never noticed it. She had gone through the little hallway into her room.

I walked in after her. The shutters were down, so that people in the rooms opposite wouldn't see her at her toilet or whatever a woman does in the privacy of her room. There was a bed over against one wall, and the other half of the room was furnished as if there wasn't a bed there. That is the usual way with these Turkish hotels.

She turned and she was playing up to me. I knew that, because I'd had it done to me before.

But when she started her playing I was looking at the telephone, and I was thinking that during that climb up four flights of stairs someone could have phoned her and told her what to expect. Someone . . . like Benny, for instance.

And suddenly I began to think about that elevator which seemed purposely out of action tonight. I realized that I hadn't seen it moving for the past hour or so and that is unusual even for this hotel. I was just wondering if there was more to it than a servant's apathy towards his job — wondering if someone didn't find it convenient to put a distance between the ground floor and, say, this one, the fourth. And then she started in earnest to play up to me.

She did some eye-fluttering, and she stood right in front of me, and she stood closer than a dame usually stands up to a stranger. She was doing it for a purpose, and in a few seconds I knew what that purpose was.

She spoke pretty good English, but it's what I call cabaret English — that is, it's been picked up and not learned in a school. She said, smilingly: 'Why do you want to speak to me?'

I stalled a bit. I don't mind an attractive judy standing up and making a play at me. Show me the man who does. It made what I was doing pleasanter, anyway.

I said: 'Look, sister, things have been happening around here tonight. I saw a girl being given the run-out from this hotel, and I'm trying to find out more about it.'

She arched those rather heavy eyebrows of hers, which looked attractive for all it might not seem so when it's put down in words. 'But why come to me? Do I know about it?'

She had moved closer to me, and she was standing almost touching me, and she was promising things with her eyes and smiling at me in a way that brings to mind that word — seductive.

She had scent on her — maybe too much scent, but I wasn't going to argue about a litre or so just then. I liked it. And I could almost feel the warmth of her body and it seemed to creep out and envelop me. And I liked that. She was feminine and very wholesome and I didn't find it a hardship to submit to her technique.

All the same I kept my mind on the job.

I heard the door handle turn cautiously behind me, through the little hall that gave on to the corridor.

I began to turn, and it was an instinctive movement because of what I had done in the way of precautions. And then I found myself caught by the arms and held, and she was holding me pretty tightly, and now there wasn't any space between our bodies.

She was looking up into my face and talking quickly, and she wasn't speaking English so perfectly now, but was mixing it with words of many languages. She was telling me that she liked me and she wanted to be my friend and — well, you know the line of patter they all give.

Only this was too quick, a little too breathless — far too sudden.

I said: 'I'm liking it, sister, but your technique's not too good.'

She didn't seem to notice the irony or at any rate be affected by it. She was pressing against me and her arms were up and around my neck and she begun to fumble with my ears — and I was wise to that, too. I could even afford to smile at her, and I did. And she was smiling at me and chattering away. Her eyes weren't slumberous any more, but trying to tell me all manner of things, though there is nothing original in what a girl's eyes can tell a man. Her face was only inches from my own, and I had that fascination which always comes over me when I see a girl's face at such close quarters. I found my eyes watching her lips, and noticing the gleam of her teeth as she spoke to me, so close to me that I could feel the warmth of her breath upon my own face.

I slid my arms around her. It's what she wanted, anyway. She was calling me: 'Beeg boy!' She was saying, in the stilted cliches of a foreigner not at home with another language: 'I like you. I could go for you in a beeg way!'

And she was smiling brilliantly up into my face, and those soft, red lips weren't more than a couple of inches away from my own willing ones. I didn't say anything to stop her act for a few minutes. If she wanted to play, Joe P. Heggy wasn't going to run away crying for mamma. I gave her squeeze for squeeze . . . and big smiles for her brilliant ones. And I know she liked it, because there's a lot of man in me — liked it even though I knew she was doing this in the line of duty.

Time passed. We stood there under the solitary electric. Then she began to change in her manner; her routine began to grow mechanical.

I knew she was beginning to be disturbed. Then this sense of perturbation began to change to alarm and even apprehension. She was on strain as she stood in my embrace.

I looked into her eyes — when they weren't trying to stare round me. I wasn't getting any colder. I was just beginning to think that B.G. could wait a long time with what he had dug up, when she started to try to push me away.

She'd finally tumbled to it that a plan had gone wrong somewhere.

I said, banteringly: 'What's eating you, sister? Don't I rate for l'amour any more?'

I didn't let her answer me. I caught her by the wrist and swung her back into my arms — picked her right off her feet and put the Heggy lips against hers. And they were so soft, so warm. She'd started this — now I wanted it to go on.

But I let her go after a while. She went

away from me, tugging at things and pulling to straighten them, as women do after they've been in a huddle. From the chair I drawled: 'They didn't come, did they?'

Because I'd known it all along, what was intended for me. She'd been tipped off to bait me — the sucker was to be bopped on the skull while enjoying her soft, red lips; some guy was to sneak in behind me while bright eyes held my attention. Only it hadn't turned out like that, and now I was letting the dame know.

She looked at me for a second, and then passion came into her face and she ran quickly into the hallway. We dead-heated for the corridor door. I wasn't having that dame throw it open and let in any apes with muscles between their ears.

I let her see what I'd done as I came into her apartment behind her. When she wasn't looking, I'd slipped home an inside bolt.

She began to abuse me then, loudly, furious because I'd been wise to her tricks. For a few seconds I thought she was going to hurl herself at me, with her reddened finger nails digging into my flesh — women can't forgive being led up the garden path, I guess.

But she didn't go for me. Maybe she saw that I wasn't disinclined for another huddle, so she stood back in the hallway and shouted blistering things at me. I got only a few words — mostly she came up with insults in unknown languages — but those few American words she knew must have been learned from the U.S. Marines.

It wasn't any good questioning the gal in that mood, so I didn't make the attempt. Anyway, I'd learned quite a lot — this slim piece of leisure moments was concerned in some plot that quite evidently had something to do with the abducted girl. I couldn't think otherwise, anyway.

I shot back the bolt quietly, then opened the door a crack. If there'd been any apes standing out there, I'd have slammed the door to pretty quickly and got on the phone to my new friend the Turkish cop.

But no silent muscle-men stood out on

that thick corridor carpet, so I gave the shrill-voiced, angry dame a wink and a 'Tch! Tch!' in best American style and went out.

I went down that corridor pretty quickly. I'd got a feeling that I wasn't going to be allowed to get away so easily. It's a nasty feeling, to have lurking in your mind the thought that someone's waiting to pounce on you as you pass and do brutal things to your cranium.

I went by those closed, silent doors like greased lightning. The hell, Joe P. Heggy doesn't believe in taking unnecessary risks!

Yet none of them opened.

No one stepped out with a blackjack.

I got out onto that balustraded area, and again the place was deserted. My fears had turned out to be groundless. Probably the apes didn't dare make an open attack for fear of being spotted . . .

I got a surprise, then. The elevator was standing before me, its gates wide open.

I thought: 'Heck, that old man's got tired of his chambermaid!' He must have been a very old man, because it wasn't midnight yet.

So I went across to where it silently awaited me, peering into the dark interior for a sign of that old man who alone seemed to know how to make the thing work.

I got another surprise, then.

I was within a few yards of that elevator when I realized something. The gate was open but there was no elevator there.

I didn't have time to get over my surprise. I was just thinking: 'The hell, what damn fool left the gates open?' Because anyone short-sighted could have stepped through the gates and gone four flights before breaking a neck.

The lights went out.

Someone came up behind me with a rush and I found myself being hurled through those open gates.

4

Miss Dunkley

I did something instinctive in the darkness that assailed me. I let myself fall forward, but I fell not down the shaft but right across it. I couldn't see where I was falling, and I didn't know what was going to happen to me. But some instinct sent me sprawling out into space, my toes digging into the landing behind me, and my hands clutching desperately for some hold opposite.

I smacked a wire rope with my left arm, but then my hands grabbed a ledge. I hung on. I was a bridge across a four-storey void.

It was about this time that I began to see again. That's how it always happens. Someone puts a light out and for an instant you're blinded. And then your eyes adjust to lesser lights — in this case light reflecting up the elevator shaft from the floors beneath — and I was able to see the predicament I was in. I didn't have long to muse over my situation. Someone took a kick at my ankles and my feet were knocked away from their toehold back on the landing. They were a nice lot of sons-of-bitches, whoever were playing games with me at that moment.

My feet and body crashed down against the far wall of the elevator, and I bruised my knees and hurt my chest and lost a lot of beauty when I smacked that wall. But I wasn't concerned about such details then. I was still hanging on, and for the moment I was alive.

I screwed my head, and started to snarl good Americanese at my assailants. But I never said what was really in my mind, because as I got up steam I saw two shadows above and behind me, and they were crashing shut the elevator gates.

I knew what those so-and-so's were up to immediately. I guess I'm kind of intuitive at times. I saw one of the shadows reach out, and I recognized the action of a man stabbing an elevator button.

At once I heard a whining sound above me, and I knew that the elevator had begun to descend.

Those shadows seemed to vanish, and then the light came on the fourth floor above me. Maybe it would have been better without that light. Then at least I would have been in ignorance of when that elevator came to brush me off my hold and send me hurtling down into the basement — and then come and sit on me with all its several tons of weight.

I think I was bawling my head off. Don't tell me any other man would have behaved differently, unless he was a jessie and fainted. I just couldn't faint then and I only wished I could.

I looked up and saw that elevator coming down faster than I had ever thought that elevator could come down. The looped cable underneath it descended past me, and then it was within a dozen feet of me . . .

And then it stopped. For a few seconds I just stared up at it, not understanding. Expecting it to start again and put Joe P. Heggy in need of an undertaker after

73

they'd scraped me out of the muck at the bottom of the elevator shaft.

I couldn't believe it — could only think: 'My God, it's broken down again!' If that was the explanation, then I'd never say anything against that old elevator again!

But I didn't stay long in a mental soliloquy. I wanted out of that hole, and quickly, before the elevator changed its mind and started to descend again.

I found there was a ledge running right round the elevator shaft, on a level with the floor that I had just quit so hastily. It was a ledge full of dirt, so that when I started to move hand over hand along it I didn't have too sure a grip at times; But right then I could have held on to it with my finger nails — even an eyebrow. Joe P. Heggy craves to live as long as any man.

I got round to that closed gate, and all the time I was staring upwards, expecting to see that elevator come whining down to crush me.

But it didn't. I never saw a nicer elevator.

It wasn't hard, when I was round under

that gate, to pull myself up onto the fourth floor and open those gates from the inside and step out onto the now well-lighted landing.

I came out, and I saw two or three people in dressing gowns and pyjamas, hovering along each of the passages that gave on to this area with its elevator and staircase.

They were mostly middle-aged and unprepossessing, in the way of middle-aged people just caught out of their beds. I didn't hold that against them. In fact, at that moment I held nothing against anyone anywhere because I was so glad to be walking a firm floor again.

I went down the stairs two or three at a time. I went into my own apartment, and I stripped off because my clothes were lined with grease where that elevator rope had touched them. I had a good wash and rid myself of the filth that had descended upon me during my couple of minutes as a prisoner in that elevator shaft. Then I put on a new set of clothes, prettied myself before a mirror, and then went down to meet B.G.

He looked at me in a way that bosses always look at employees who haven't quite pleased them. His flat pancake face cracked open and I knew from the start that he was trying to show off before the little dame who was still hovering round him.

He rapped: 'Heggy, what have you been doing? Didn't I hear you yelling up above just now?'

I said: 'I was yelling. So what?'

That question floored him.

He knew that if he tried to take the rise out of Joe P. Heggy he was likely to end up squashed, and I could see that he didn't want that, not in front of that export from austerity Britain.

So he changed his tune a bit, and asked: 'What were you doing? I mean, why were you creating like that?'

I looked coldly at him and told him: 'I was taking my exercises inside the elevator shaft, and, the damn' thing started to come down on me.'

The sap started to shush me. He looked significantly at the timid little soul at his elbow and said quickly:

'Not so much of the language, Heggy.'

I looked into that timid dame's face, and I said: 'If a damn harms a lady, she oughtn't to be on this earth.' I was in that kind of mood, you see. I'd been near to death, and a little thing like a damn didn't rate high in my opinion of the sins of the world. What did rankle was a shove in the back, which had nearly put an end to a man I care for more than anyone else on earth. Me. Joe P. Heggy.

B.G. didn't know what I was talking about and didn't believe me, anyway. He hadn't even noticed my quick change of clothes, and he started to give orders to impress the little dame.

He said: 'Miss Dunkley is coming with us to the *Gazino*, Heggy.'

I slapped my key on the desk for Benny to hook up for when I returned. I looked at B.G. and then at the bashful, mousy-haired little dame, and I said, archly: 'Now, I wonder what's taken her mind off ruins?'

She fluttered in an excess of embarrassment. B.G. thought I was being rude, and he became excessively formal and polite.

'Perhaps I should introduce you. Miss Dunkley, this is an assistant — '

' — a nursemaid and bodyguard!' I interrupted sourly.

'An assistant,' the fat slob said viciously, 'called Heggy. Mr. Heggy, allow me to introduce you to — '

'Okay, okay,' I interposed. 'I know what comes next. Mr. Heggy meet Miss Dunkley.' I gave her a flick of the Heggy paw, and said: 'Hyar, babe. How's Miss Dunk?'

It didn't go down at all well with B.G. But right then I was still trying to take it out of someone for the shaking up I had gone through. B.G. was as good as anyone to rile, right at that moment.

He yammered at me all the way out until we got a taxi. Then he stopped talking because no one can talk coherently in an Istanbul taxi. They're driven by madmen possessed of the finest motoring skill in the world. The fittest only survive, and my theory is that even the best can't live long as an Istanbul taxi-driver.

We got thrown about a lot together in

the back of that cab and I was the only one who did any bellyaching.

When we got out at the *Gazino*, we sorted ourselves out and gave each other back the right arms and legs, which had got all tied up in the journey over the hill.

The little dame went ahead. I saw her going towards the bright lights that marked the entrance to the *Gazino*, and then I noticed that B.G. was not going after her, but was standing there looking after her small, rather shrinking little form.

I looked at B.G., and then said: 'Give, brother, give. What's biting you?'

His big head turned and he looked at me through his glasses and then he turned his head again and looked after the little dame. And his expression was dazed, like a man who has suffered a shock.

I grabbed him by the elbow, and dug in painfully through his fat. I don't like my questions being ignored by bosses. I said: 'I asked you a question?'

That seemed to bring him out of his trance and he dragged his arm away from me and rubbed it painfully. But he seemed so astonished that he didn't even appear to bear resentment towards me because of the pain of that grip which had been intentionally painful.

He just looked at me, and then I heard him mutter:

'I wouldn't have believed it. My God, no I wouldn't!'

I yammered: 'For Pete's sake, what wouldn't you have believed?'

But he didn't answer that question; he went slowly towards that little dame, and it seemed to me almost that he went in a circling movement, as if to keep a yard or two distance from her, and he was staring at her all the time through his eight-sided glasses.

Little Miss Dunkley turned and smiled at him, and she was all a-flutter and dropping her eyes and going pink with confusion. She looked painfully out of this world, and it was a pose — though unintentional, of course — which seemed to appeal to big, fat B.G. Me, I like 'em worldly.

I saw B.G. start to pull himself together

again. I even saw him pull his stomach in a couple of yards, and then he said, but not really to any audience but rather to himself: 'It must have been an accident.' And then he was beaming on the little London woman and going flat out to impress her again.

Right then, I saw a man and I went across to him and I said a few words in his ear. He was a complete stranger to me, but I knew he was the man whose ear I had been looking for.

He was a Turk. He was dressed in the light suiting which the middle-class Turk adopts for summer wear, when he goes out nights. He was a rather stolid-looking, impassive man, approaching my own height — which means he was pretty big. I planted myself slap in front of him as he came out from a taxi just drawn up behind the one we'd quit. And I said to him: 'Brother, you get word through to that boss of yours, and tell him they've tried to sort me out already.'

The man looked at me. He didn't say anything, and his rather heavy face didn't register anything, either.

So I went on: 'You tell him that a couple of rubes tried to drop me down an elevator shaft. Tell him I've got an idea that some of the people we're looking for are staying in that hotel.'

That's what I told him, and only when I finished did I realize what I had done . . .

I hadn't mentioned the girl who was passing off as Marie Konti.

He looked at me, and then in not very good English he said: 'Excuse? I do not understand, effendi?'

I gave him a flip of my paw to show my contempt for the attempted bluff. When it comes to bluffing you've got to go to a land where you're brought up with a deck of poker cards in your hand.

I was sure of myself. This was the guy who had been getting callouses on his backside on that visitors' bench in the hotel foyer. I'd guessed there would be someone around after what the police officer had told me, and I'd been looking for him. I wanted to get a message through to that husky capable young officer.

I think this Turk had been a little afraid that I, a touchy American national, might have been angry to have discovered a police agent following me. But now he must have gathered that I wasn't. In fact, I was darned glad.

I said: 'Look, brother, you go off and phone that report through and get your chief to comb that hotel again, while I go in and get myself round a meal and a couple of bottles. I'll be in there when you come back.'

He got it at once that I was willing to play along with the police.

He didn't waste words, that fellow; he just nodded and went quickly into the *Gazino* and I knew he was on his way to find a phone.

We never went into the *Gazino*. One minute later we were piling into a taxi again.

I'd started to go after B.G. and his one-woman admiration-society when I saw that big pancake face of his come back round the entrance and I realized that he was heading out and bringing a bewildered little dame with him.

His face was flushed, and his eyes uneasy, and I knew he'd seen something that had put a scare up him. So I stood across the sidewalk slap in front of him and demanded: 'Where are you heading, B.G.? I thought we were going to eat in the *Gazino*?'

He said, quickly: 'I've changed my mind. I've just remembered a place which will please Miss Dunkley more.'

But he didn't kid me. He was running out on something, and I wanted to know what it was. He wouldn't tell me and I knew he was ashamed of his fear, and wasn't going to reveal it in front of little Dunk. He was doing a lot of talking and extolling the virtues of the place he had it in mind to visit.

He argued: 'Miss Dunkley has seen places like the *Gazino* before.'

Miss Dunkley looked astonished, as if in fact she had never been to a place like the *Gazino*. 'I think she'd much prefer to see something more native.'

Miss Dunkley nodded very quickly several times, as if to convey how clever he was in understanding her wishes. But I thought that when she looked over her shoulder at the bright lights of the *Gazino* she looked very wistful, as if she'd have liked to have seen Istanbul's No. 1 nighterie.

I did some wistful looking myself, too. Because the *Gazino's* a place worth visiting any evening. It's the biggest of Istanbul's places of entertainment; and it is built on a steep hillside overlooking the Bosphorus, so that in summer you dine out in the moonlight under a starry sky, on terraces brilliantly illuminated, while a good orchestra plays for dancing and the best cabaret acts in the Middle East are put on for the diners. I could hear a lilting Samba and it made my feet itch and I wanted to go inside and join the audience I knew to be there already — because it was there every night of the week.

You see the loveliest of women at the *Gazino*. They dress superbly, and they are of every race under the sun. They look . . . exotic . . . alluring.

Though you can't go up and ask a dame to dance unless you know her family, but you can look at them and that's something, anyway. It makes the lobster thermidor taste all the better.

We went on to the street arguing, but for once the boss was in a mood to stand up to my argument, and I began to realize that something had scared the pants off him. I couldn't make it out, but I had to do as I was told. So I got into that taxi with him, and heard him give an address to the driver. The only trouble was, without intending to I had ditched my police shadow, and I felt that mightn't be a good thing, especially because the address that big slob had given the driver was in a rough quarter of Istanbul.

However, there was nothing I could do about it. B.G. was running away from something, and he was in the mood to try to impress little Miss Dunk.

I said, inside the taxi as it lurched away: 'Maybe Achmet's joint isn't the kind of place to take Lavinia.' He looked at me, and I caught the expression on his face as we slid away from the bright lights in front of the *Gazino*. He said: 'Lavinia?'

Evidently the sap hadn't got around to

her first name yet. That was slow of the boss. I'd give him a few tips when I felt inclined.

We slid into darkness and were all held together at a corner. I said, taking the dame's elbow out of my ear: 'That's Miss Dunkley, B.G. Isn't it, Lavinia?'

She murmured something. I went on: 'It's a mouthful. We'll call her Lav for short from now on.'

I heard B.G.'s shocked exclamation in the darkness.

'You'll do no such thing. Dammit, Heggy, you go too far. That's no way to talk to a lady.' I just took no notice of him. The hell, what was undignified about that?

We went down the steep cobbled hill through the business quarter to the Galata Bridge, which spanned the Golden Horn. We were tossed around more than considerably, which is what you expect from a Turkish driver. But we stayed alive long enough to reach our destination and for B.G. to get his fat hands into his hip pocket and find the exorbitant fee which every Turkish taxi driver demands of an

American. He always gets it, too, because after a ride in a Turkish taxi no one is ever inclined to argue with the man who has brought them so near to death so many times. I guess that's the psychology of taxi-driving in Istanbul . . .

We were down in the old quarter of the town now, where tourists usually come in groups because there is a sinister quality about this sector of old Istanbul.

We got out of that taxi along with our bruises, and then I realized that B.G.'s hand was trembling so much he could hardly get out his money to pay that taxi-driver. We began to walk towards the nighterie, and in the lights over the entrance I realized that B.G.'s big fat face was hot and flushed. I heard him exclaim: 'It wasn't an accident, Heggy!' And there was agony in his voice and horror.

He didn't say any more, because Lavinia Dunkley was demurely waiting for him on the sidewalk.

5

American Defilers

By now I was getting to such a state that I wanted to stand where I was and shout: 'For God's sake, someone explain some of these mysteries to me!'

There was that shemozzle back at the hotel, and now there was B.G. starting up a mystery all of his own. No one would tell me anything, and it didn't do my libido any good to be in this state of frustration.

I know I was yammering, raising my voice and asking questions as we went into Achmet's. But B.G. was ignoring me, and he even seemed to turn his fat shoulder towards me, as if he didn't want to hear what I was saying. He was agitated and kept rubbing at those useless glasses of his, and I couldn't understand it at all.

Achmet's is another of these 'au plein

air' establishments, which abound in this city of Istanbul. The only difference between it and the *Gazino*, in fact, was that the place was smaller, they got a more raffish type of patron, and the band, to my Western ears, was lousy. It was a show place for tourists, and a bit overdone at that. Especially they overdid it when they brought on their Turkish women singers.

These belonged to the old school, and the fatter they were the more they went down with an audience just beginning to realize that Betty Grable had everything, though she weighed less than half these screaming dames.

One was screaming now. It was hideous, but her compatriots were enraptured and gave her a big hand when she took her chins away from an unnecessary microphone. Even B.G. seemed to wince at the volume of sound, but the little woman smiled bravely and gave out she was enjoying the native singing.

We got a table, and ordered supper. I ordered the drinks, and made it a rush order because I felt in need of them. I wasn't too happy in this joint, anyway, because I thought that some of the types weren't so much raffish as sinister, and I kept looking round at them and trying to spot any trouble if it was coming.

Trouble blew in by the main entrance a few minutes later. I wasn't looking that way, but B.G. was and I saw his fleshy jaw drop almost onto his chest and an agonised look came into his little eyes. Almost I felt his fat hulk trembling, and I turned to see what was agitating the boss.

Five men were threading their way through the tables towards us from the entrance. They were coming rather quickly, rather roughly, so that Achmet's patrons looked up at them as they went by, and the waiters turned to watch them. They were men looking for trouble, and they were looking straight at the quivering B.G.

I sighed, and massaged my fists. Trouble was where my job began. My function was a little different here, in Europe, but when trouble threatened the boss that was where I had to step in.

That's why he gave me my monthly paycheck.

That little London woman could feel that something was wrong, that something threatened, and her anxious little face turned from B.G.'s to mine. I tried to reassure her. I said: 'If anyone gets killed, Lav,' — I nodded towards the boss — 'there's the corpus delecti.'

B.G. seemed to stiffen in an agonised manner when he heard my caustic humour, but this was no time to quarrel with his only friend. He said nothing, but his eyes lifted as the leader of that quintet came over to him.

He was a big hairy ape, and ginger with it. He was American, like the other boys with him. His eyes were cold and contemptuous as he looked at B.G., and his voice was even colder, even more contemptuous. He said: 'We saw you!' — witheringly. 'You ducked away when you saw us at the *Gazino*, didn't you? But we saw you, and came after you, for we reckon no boss should be ashamed to be in the same place as his men.'

I was standing now. It paid to be on

your feet when that quintet of huskies was around late enough at night for them to have had a skinful. And they had been drinking.

That ginger ape was Marty Dooley. He was sometimes known as the Show Boss, because he managed and publicised every export project of Gissenheim's. Behind him, slim, dark, smiling, was Dwight Laite, Gissenheim's export sales chief, and with him was Gorby Tuhlman who was Boss Engineer, whose duty it was to see that Gissenheim's dirt-shifters shifted dirt at their peak of efficiency. Harry Sauer, his assistant, was with him and he looked pretty well gone, and so did Tony Geratta, our Middle East sales rep.

They were a wild bunch, but there wasn't any malice in them. They just had a queer sense of humour, and their idea of a night out was to get around a few bottles and then plague the hell out of the boss's son. For a long time I'd wondered why even B.G. had let 'em get away with it, and then I'd found that they had a hold on him. They were quite cheerful about it and would tell you what that hold was if you asked — B.G. had made some damn' fool proviso in a contract which could have cost the firm a quarter of a million if Dwight Laite hadn't spotted it and done some smart work to cover them. They could get away with murder after that, because if B.G. tried any tricks with them, they just up and threatened to tell the old man what a fool son he'd brought into the world.

The others came up and swayed around the table and had a gawk at B.G.'s supreme effort towards dissipation. They were inclined to be crude in their humour.

B.G. had begun to put on the ice and try to freeze them out, but it didn't work. Marty kept yammering for an introduction to B.G.'s girlfriend. It made little Dunk blush, and it got B.G. all hot under the collar.

I wasn't watching these reactions very closely just then, because I was looking towards the entrance once more, and there was something there that was making me think. Another party had entered the nighterie, and they looked as out of place in it as we did. They were big, solid-muscled men, rather sleekly dressed, and yet looking a bit out of place in their party suits. But I was thinking, as I looked at them, that any two of these boys could have been those apes down in the alley who had taken away the pyjama-clad girl.

I think my suspicions were aroused from the start, because as they came in each of them looked round the restaurant and seemed in turn to meet my eyes. After that they went to a table and never once appeared to look in my direction at all. Don't think it ego, but I felt that to be unnatural, in view of the interest our table was attracting from the surrounding patrons.

I came back to my own party as waiters tried tactfully to get the boys into chairs at a table adjoining ours. Plainly the boys were drunk and ripe for mischief, and were already stirring things up for their boss.

B.G. apparently hadn't introduced the English piece of frumpery, so I obliged, thinking that it might quiet down the boys and get them in their seats. I said: 'This is Lav, boys. If she knew what a Casanova she was sitting next to, she'd get the hell out of this place pretty quick, I can tell you.'

B.G. looked nastily at me, but at least it got those boys into their chairs at the next table, and that was something. Only, it didn't stop their voices.

Marty was especially drunk, and everything he said brought hiccups of delight from Harry Sauer and Tony Geratta. They were almost in the mood to giggle at anything, though. Marty bawled out, in a voice loud enough for half the restaurant to hear: 'Li'l B.G.'s found a soul-mate at last.' He looked round at his companions with drunken solemnity, and said: 'All these years he's been saving the Gissenheim torso for the moment when the right li'l woman came along. And now — she's got it!'

It made B.G. blush and blink behind his glasses, because Marty was touching him in a tender place. I tell you that B.G. had more complexes and inhibitions and wrong slants on life than any fifteen men

I've ever met. He didn't believe in enjoying himself. Leastways, that's how it looked to us.

For instance he used to click his tongue when we talked about the good times we had with the gals we met in these countries to which we travelled. He used to sit apart and look as if he wasn't listening, but we all knew that his ears were flapping just the same. And one day he had tried to crush us, by telling us what an example he was setting. He was avoiding women, he had told us, because he was saving himself for the moment when the right woman came into his life.

The boys had never forgotten that statement — and they'd never let B.G. forget it, either. Now Marty began crudely to tell Lavinia what a paragon she had picked up, and didn't she think she was lucky to have met up with a virgin, so far from home? Yeah, he used that word; and while a woman will take a court action if she isn't acclaimed virgo intacta, a man hates to carry the label.

Anyway, he doesn't like the fact proclaimed in public.

B.G. looked at me in an agonised manner. He wanted me to do something, but short of going across and knocking their teeth out I didn't see what a trouble-buster could do for him. I told him so. He hung onto my words so that he wouldn't hear the wicked, drawling voice of Dwight Laite, who was saying things now.

Then Harry Sauer got into trouble. One of the girls came across to their table. You know the kind I mean. All lips and smiles and a waggle of come-hither hips. There are always a few in these joints, especially since tired American businessmen began to pour into the country on construction and other jobs.

Harry, who's young and a nice boy, leered up at her and gave her the 'Hyar, babe!' She didn't tell him, but she halted by his side and smiled encouragingly at the Americano. Harry promptly reached out to pull her down on to his knee or do something like he'd seen on the movies.

That girl didn't mind. In fact that's what that girl wanted, because it was her trade. She had to go through the performance, of course, of struggling a little, but you expect that and everybody knows it doesn't mean a thing. Harry knew it, and he didn't let up.

But someone in the audience did object. Because it was an audience now, because there was quite a lot of noise going on from Harry's table.

Most of the patrons were, I suspect, mildly interested by the Americans, because after all there wasn't much untoward in their behaviour. What I mean is, extrovert Americans behave like that wherever they go — it's a demonstration of a superiority complex engendered by a pocketful of almighty dollars, and that's a mighty good sentence by Joe P. Heggy.

But someone began to shout angrily, and though I didn't know a word of what was being said, I guessed what the contents of those shouted sentences were. It was an appeal to racial hatred. Yeah, I mean it. It keeps happening, wherever you get the haves consorting with people who haven't quite as much.

In a moment that place was in an uproar. Suddenly lots of people decided to become angry with the Americanos who behaved arrogantly in public and offered insults to their womenfolk. The fact that the woman in question was probably Greek or Italian or some other nationality (their kind are rarely Turkish in Turkey) and she wasn't averse to being 'insulted', didn't register through their temper.

Human psychology being what it is, all at once it seemed that Achmet's open-air restaurant became suddenly violently anti-American. Men grew heated and rose from their tables, and we saw their brown, angry eyes turned towards us. Not to be backward, a few of the ladies threw in a lot of high-pitched screaming.

A harassed proprietor came running down among the tables with his hands uplifted. He didn't want to offend his normal patrons, but these visiting Americans brought very good additional business to his restaurant. He wanted his cake and he wanted to eat it.

I was sitting back in my chair watching proceedings and I suppose I looked sour and cynical. I'd been through it all before in other parts of the world. But then my eyes went across to where that quartet of big slobs were sitting. For it was from this table the first angry cry had gone up against the American defilers of their womanhood. They'd started this ruckus, and I got the feeling that they had started it deliberately.

I kept my eyes on them, and they were watching me all the time now — not the other members of my party, I was sure, just . . . me.

Then a scuffle started. I suppose it was funny to watch how it began. The girl who had been 'insulted' had jumped up in indignation from Harry's knee and was chattering angrily at her would-be protectors. The heck, she was saying, you keep to your own business and leave me to mine!

But chivalrous manhood couldn't be so ungallant. It was suddenly determined to save this girl from the insults of the foreigner. A little fellow who ought to have known better had got himself so excited that suddenly he came jumping forward in a flurry of fists and feet and smacked Harry so hard on the nose that poor Harry went crashing back out of his chair.

That was the signal for more action. Suddenly a lot of frustrated men thought it a good thing to dissipate some of their frustration in the form of violent energy expended on the damn' foreigners. Some of the younger show-offs came forward to acquit themselves before the eyes of their lovelies. The Turkish male is normally rather a jolly, good-humoured man, but he can get dramatic especially when there is a woman sitting around to applaud his masculine abilities.

There was a glorious shindig. Marty clouted the angry little man who had bloodied Harry's face, and then a couple of young Turks grabbed Marty and did a lot of painful things to him. The table went over and Tony Geratta went with it. He stayed where he was on the floor and he was a wise man because he wasn't in any condition to add to the fighting. Waiters came rushing up behind a shrieking, frantic proprietor, desperately striving to separate the contestants.

Marty, Dwight and Gorby were fighting a battle against an increasing number of irate Turkish patrons. Then Harry staggered back into the fray, and he felt sore and he got wicked with a chair.

Oh, I forgot, I was in it, too. I just found myself going in on the side of my buddies. It's a thing you do and you don't question the rights or wrongs attached to the cause of your friends at such times.

Someone loomed up and pushed my nose a couple of inches into my skull. I thought there was an idea back of that and I smacked him so hard his nose went right in among his sinuses, or whatever is back of a Turk's nose. Then someone jumped me and we went down and started rolling among the legs of the struggling fighters around the overturned tables. It was hot work, and I was sweating and gasping and lashing out furiously.

Somehow I got away from the couple of Turks who were trying to cave my chest in. I had to use knees and elbows to do it, as I couldn't have stood much more of that punishment on the ground. So I used them.

When I got to my feet and looked at the excited faces converging in on us from all directions, I knew I was supporting a lost cause. I suddenly remembered I was a nervous man and decided to beat it. I picked Tony Geratta up and slung him over my shoulder. And then I charged towards the entrance of the nighterie. Back of me Marty and the others must have got the same idea. I heard them trying to fight their way out, but they would never have done it if those waiters hadn't dug in and given them a hand.

I started to climb the steps, which gave on to the winter quarters of the nightclub. Then I saw B.G. ahead of me. He was sprinting so fast he looked like a greyhound — though a damn fat greyhound at that. Right behind him tagged little Miss Dunkley. I didn't blame her.

Neither of them had the material of fighters within them.

But even at that moment I got a queer idea.

It looked to me, not that Lavinia was running out on the brawl, but was determinedly chasing after big, fat B.G.

I didn't have time to speculate. The uproar behind me was frantic now, and almost every woman in the place was giving way to hysteria, and indignant males were grouped together and shouting after the Americanos who came to upset things. The Americanos were climbing the steps after me, and they looked considerably battered and their clothes were torn and soiled and hung in disorder about them. And yet they seemed cheerful enough. All except Gorby Tuhlman, who was inclined to stand on his rights.

'The hell,' he kept saying. 'We didn't start anything. I'm going to see the ambassador about this. The hell, they can't treat me like that!'

But they could, and by the look of it they were ready to treat us again. So, ushered out by a circle of waiters, and a manager who was trying to gloss over the incident, we went walking out into the night air.

But just before we left that restaurant in the garden I looked towards a table where four impassive-faced huskies had been sitting, but their chairs were empty.

I dumped Tony into the arms of Marty and Dwight. I said: 'You got him like that; you get him to bed. I can't play Nurse Nellie to all the infants around here.'

So I went out of that nightery ahead of the boys. I saw B.G. trembling out on the sidewalk under the shaded lights that decorated the entrance to Achmet's. He had been waving for a taxi, and I could see one lurching up in the distance. Little Miss Dunkley was standing near to him, and it seemed to me that B.G. was trying to keep a distance between himself and the frail little woman.

I went out, the sound of triumphant Turkish manhood still loud in my ears through the swinging door of the nightery. I was looking at little Miss Dunkley. She had changed considerably, and I found myself marvelling at the change right then. If I hadn't known that she'd only got outside a small glass of wine at the table in Achmet's, I'd have thought her to be excited by alcohol. She seemed younger. She was not a frail-looking wisp of a woman any longer. Instead she had rather a kind of reckless air, as if she had burnt her boats and was glad she had done so. The French have a word for her manner and it's sufficiently English to be understood. The word is — *abandon*.

I looked into her bright — astonishingly bright — eyes and her flushed face and I thought: 'There's still a lot of life in the old girl yet!' Though she didn't look old — she didn't even look middle-aged, now. A night out was doing Lavinia a whole lot of good. So I couldn't understand why B.G. was manoeuvring to keep away from her. He had liked Lavinia in her old-maidishness; why didn't he appreciate her more now she was coming out of her shell?

The taxi came screaming to a violent halt. That was accepted taxi practice in Istanbul, but it always scared the life out of me. That gave B.G. a chance to whisper in my ear, because Lavinia just naturally went and stood by the taxi. I turned when he came quickly up to me, and I saw the agitation on his fat face and the trembling of his hands. I said: 'What in heck's name's bitten you, B.G.?'

I heard his whisper, and it was the voice of sheer agony. He said: 'Oh, my God. You've got to do something, Heggy. Don't forget, you're paid to protect me!'

I just stared at the sap, wondering if he was in his right mind.

He went on, in those quick jumpy sentences: 'Don't you see, Heggy? It's — her!' He was polishing his glasses again in agitation. 'She's hot!'

My eyes swivelled towards that little woman. She was looking at B.G. with a smile on her face, and it reminded me of some smiles I had seen in the past.

I began to laugh. I said crudely: 'What was she doing to you in the taxi before?'

He seemed to blush. He muttered: 'That's it, Heggy. All the time she was trying to hold on to me and get close to me.' His eyes looked agonised again. 'You've got to keep her from me. I don't like this, I tell you!'

Evidently Lavinia wasn't the right

woman for B.G.! Then I heard sounds behind as if the boys had met up with more trouble in the entrance hall of Achmet's. I had no sympathy with B.G.'s inhibitions. I saw that Lavinia had ducked inside the taxi, and now I put my hand on B.G.'s fat back and pushed him in after her. I slammed the door on him, and shouted the name of the hotel, and the taxi went jumping away.

The last thing I saw was B.G.'s fat face looking in terror at me through the taxi window.

So I went back to tell the boys about it, because it seemed the funniest thing since Bob Hope. They'd rib that poor devil raw during the next six months over this incident, because none of them would understand why a man should want to run away from a perfectly willing female . . .

An arm reached out from the decorative bushes that flanked the entrance to Achmet's. I was looking through the glass doors at Marty and the others, who were having an argument with some tough-looking waiters over the bill, but I just caught a glimpse of that arm reaching towards me.

I saw it too late. That hand grabbed me by the coat sleeve and I was yanked in among those bushes. Then someone took the Mosque of Omar and smacked me on the head with it, and I was — out!

6

Almost a Corpse

I was out, but for only a fraction of time.
The Heggy skull has had many things
bounced against it, and it has grown
somewhat thick and impervious to assault
in consequence.

I think that within a couple of seconds,
in fact, I began to recover some of my
faculties. I remember, for some curious
reason, coming out of my momentary
unconsciousness with the thought: 'Now,
why didn't I tell the cops about that gal
who tried to take me for a sucker in her
apartment?' And I remember thinking
that it was against the Heggy tradition to
get a dame into trouble, even though she
had had rather unpleasant plans for J.P.H.

But thoughts of that moment with the
girl vanished swiftly. I found myself being
dragged by the arms out from the bushes.
I remember that my toes were trailing — I

111

was as far out as that. And I remember deciding to be foxy, to give myself time to get over that crack on the skull. I let my toes drag.

I hadn't any doubts as to the identity of my assailants. These weren't local thugs out to take my pocket-book, I knew. If that was all they wanted, they would have grabbed my wad under cover of the shrubbery and beat it. These boys were the flat-faced apes who had started the ruckus in Achmet's. They had been waiting for me and they wanted *me*, not my dough.

I heard grunting sounds as they pulled my big weight along. Then I heard Marty's voice. And then a crash of glass, and I thought: 'The boys have seen me, and they've walked through the door because they hadn't time to open it.'

So I decided to come out of my 'coma' pretty quickly.

I lifted my head, and looked into blazing headlights, which were tearing towards us. I jumped onto my feet and wrestled with my captors. I knew what that approaching car meant. I was to be taken for a ride. Once they got me inside, I'd be well and truly a prisoner.

For it seemed to me that I recognized that big sedan as the kidnap car that had waltzed off with the girl in pyjamas. I wasn't going in that car. I tore into those apes and I was snarling and saying nasty things; and trying to beat the heads off them. I heard Marty shouting, but they'd got themselves tangled up with Tony Geratta who was still not able to stand, and couldn't follow for a few vital seconds.

They were solid monkeys, and my fists didn't make much impression on them. They stood around me, snarling back and chopping and battering at me, and I took an awful lot of punishment and my head wasn't in a condition to receive it. Then one of the apes slugged me and I just managed to get my shoulder in the way of the blow, so that it only glanced onto my cheekbone, but it sent me staggering out of the fight.

I went down in a sideways fall, right in front of that kidnap car, and I'll swear the driver accelerated and tried to run me down. Perhaps that would have been just as convenient to my would-be kidnappers as Joe P. Heggy alive. An accident is sometimes a convenient way of silencing a blabbermouth.

It never got within a yard of Joe P. Heggy. I've dodged too much traffic around Fifth Avenue to be caught by any car driver. I got up onto one hand and took a dive beyond the car, and that gave me a chance to get away from those big, tough apes.

That glossy, imported sedan screamed to a halt when the driver saw he had missed me, and that put the bulk of the car between me and the apes. So I started to run for it, and I got a lead because the apes had to go round the car, and that was all in my favour.

I didn't know where I was going, but I knew I wasn't staying anywhere near that car which might be a hearse for Joe P. Heggy. True, I had friends only a few yards away from that car, but I couldn't depend on them, and I wasn't going to risk being snatched right from under their noses.

So I ran for it. My head was spinning, and there was blood running down from my face where the Heggy nose bled. There was a kind of square in front of Achmet's, and on the other side were tall, black warehouse-like buildings, designed on the Victorian English style. I got across that moonlit square, and I heard the roar of the sedan as it started up and came curving round to head me off.

The sonovabitch tried to run me down again, but my head was clearing and I was faster on my feet now. I jumped for it at the last moment, but his wing caught my foot and tipped me in a long roll, smack up against a warehouse wall. I was taking a lot of punishment that night, but just then I didn't seem to be noticing it. I guess that always happens when there's something mighty important at stake — your life.

I picked myself up and I didn't stop to count the bruises. I saw four hulking apes racing across that moonlit square towards me, and I had time to notice that even then their faces still retained that curiously impassive expression I had noticed when first they entered Achmet's.

I wheeled and went plunging down an alley too narrow for that sedan to follow. But the apes could, and I heard the smack of their shoes upon the cobbled way.

I didn't hear Marty or the other boys' voices after that. I guessed that distance and the alcoholic load they were carrying must have been a handicap.

I was on my own.

I went down that alley like a man trying to make the home base. I'd no doubts in my mind as to the intentions of those apes behind me. Someone had tried to rub me out only a few hours before, and I guessed these birds had similar intentions. I couldn't understand why — not altogether — because being witness to an abduction didn't seem to warrant such drastic measures.

But I kept running. That alley gave out onto another alley, and that gave out onto yet another alley. It was the commercial quarter of Istanbul, with offices and warehouses leading down to the wharves. At this time of night it was deserted, and there wasn't a light in any of the buildings, and I ran along shadowy, cobbled ways with four silent killers racing to catch up with me.

The moon glowed brilliantly white and clear, so that I ran alternately in the deepest of shadow and then into the whiteness of near daylight.

Then I got a bit of luck. I dodged right, down yet another alley, and then turned suddenly left through a gateway and ran down an open passageway which led between two buildings. I heard the apes go padding swiftly past the entrance to that passage.

Though they must have discovered their mistake within seconds and come back and found that open doorway. But this gave me the start I needed.

I made the most of it. I ran more carefully now, because I didn't have any more wind left, and I moved silently from shadow to shadow, and tried to steal away from my enemies in that manner.

I could hear them behind me, and then I heard someone running down an alleyway parallel to the one I was in, and I guessed they had split up and were looking for me. And then I got an idea that someone was right at the end of this moonlit alley, this canyon between high, dark warehouse buildings.

I halted in the deepest of shadows and watched.

Someone came into view right at the end of the alley. It was no use going that way any more.

Then I saw a movement from an alleyway almost opposite me, and it put an end to thoughts of escape down that side turning.

A sound from behind brought my head swivelling round. The other two apes had planted themselves across the alley behind me. I was trapped. Then the apes began to walk towards me, all except the rube in the side turning almost abreast of me.

I saw those big hulking shapes move slowly down towards each other, watching, and crouching in the manner of men who expect sudden action. They weren't taking any chances, and there wasn't a shadow in a doorway or behind any of the piles of junk, which littered the alleyway left unexamined.

They were coming nearer, and I caught a glimpse of metal in the hand of the ape coming from my right. I was in a worse position than if I'd stopped to fight it out by the entrance to Achmet's. Here were no friends. Here they could do what they wanted to me.

And I knew what they wanted.

There was a shutter to my right hand. It was over a window, and I had a suspicion there wouldn't be any glass at the back of it, because they don't run to a lot of glass in the warehouses alongside the waterfront.

So I put my fingers between a crack where two shutters joined. I reckon those shutters were dry and warped from long years in the brilliant Turkish sunshine, and when I threw all my weight into tugging at them, they came apart with astonishing ease.

But they made an almighty noise.

At the sound of tearing wood, all four apes came leaping towards me. One of the shutters came apart from its hinges and I felt its weight in my hands. I turned and tossed it right into the face of the rube streaking towards me from the turning opposite. And then I pulled myself into that dark void of a window, thanking heaven there were no bars in position, as so often is the case.

I found myself standing in a blackness that was profound after the brilliant moonlight out in the alley. I kept moving, though, because I knew those apes were jumping towards the window, and I didn't want to be an experiment for that knife in one of their hands. I walked away, but then gathered speed as my eyes became accustomed to the gloom. Some light was coming in from unshuttered windows high above me. I was in some sort of chemical factory, among rows of silent vats, huge wooden tubs, each of which would hold a couple of thousand gallons of liquid. There were shafts and pulleys and cross-beltings and all the paraphernalia of a chemical factory.

There was also the stink of flat, sour acid — the odour of chemicals left exposed in those vats and in the iron tanks, which I began to see rearing in the distance.

I began to run, and I found the floor slippery with slime, and I went over and ruined another good suit that night. I didn't count the cost, though, and went hell-for-leather down among those vats. Back of me I heard grunts as big men levered themselves through the narrow space of that broken-shuttered window.

Someone took a bang at me with a gun, then, and I went skittering away under the platform, which supported the vats. Joe P. Heggy didn't want a verdict of 'Death by lead poisoning'.

Right then I could have done with a police shadow. But there was no one inside that chemical factory to help me except Joe P. Heggy.

For about five minutes we played a grim game of hide and seek. They seemed prepared to use their guns, here inside that big dark cavernous chemical factory, and once or twice I saw red flame in the darkness and lead came spinning towards me.

I kept clambering over slimy, rusty

pipes underneath vats, which dripped unpleasantly upon me. I ducked between tanks that stank of acid, and raced silently along metal catwalks where big egg-shaped pressure vessels were arranged.

I didn't know where I was going; all I knew was that those four apes were systematically searching through that factory for me and I was intent on keeping one jump ahead of them.

It was a long building, and there were stairs that led upwards, but I didn't dare take to them for fear of being trapped. I kept on the ground level and I tried to make progress in a straight line, so that I wouldn't get lost and run into any of those murderous monkeys in the dark.

All at once I found myself staring at the head of a long, sloping, covered passageway, which was moonlit where beams strayed in through cracks in the corrugated metal structure. I got the stink of water then — the smell you get whenever you come near to docks and wharves. I went down that sloping passageway, because in any event I had nowhere else to go. The apes were right behind me, and were rapidly closing in on me.

I ran like the wind down that long straight corridor, and all the time I expected to feel something go thunk into my body — then I'd feel pain and go sprawling and I'd hear the follow-up sound of a revolver firing. And then Joe P. Heggy would be up among the angels . . . maybe.

I must have got the Heggy legs working overtime because I got almost to the end of that shadowy passageway before a hoarse shout from behind told me that I had been sighted. Someone did blast off at me then, but it was probably difficult to see me among the shadows and the bullet hit a metal wall and seemed to scream in reproach past my left ear.

Then I came out of that passageway and into the full light of the moon, just as I heard the heavy thud of those apes racing after me. I went on running. The moonlight was so bright after the half-light of the last five minutes that it seemed almost to hurt.

I could see everything. I could see the rising mountainside upon which the newer, fashionable residential quarter of Istanbul is built. There were lights everywhere, and neons glowed colourfully, and headlights of cars came sweeping round the bending roads and gave movement to the scene. At the foot of the hill was mostly shadows, because there began the commercial sector of the north bank of the Horn. And between me and that shadowy shore was the bright glistening wave-dappled waters of the fabulous Golden Horn.

I kept running towards the water, across a wide concrete wharf, which ended abruptly by the water's edge — as wharves have a habit of doing. I didn't turn left and I didn't right, because there didn't seem any sense in turning, because there seemed no way of escape that way. On either side of me were ranged rows of steel drums, mighty things weighing nearly half a ton each when filled, as I knew from my work with Gissenheims. They flanked it, and were effective barriers to escape along the wharf to the right and left of me. And in effect they channelled me towards the front of the wharf.

I didn't like it, legging it like fury across that moonlit staging, but again I had no alternative. I kept running and I expected yet again to get a bullet in my back.

I heard the apes come running out onto the wharf, but they didn't open fire.

Then the thought occurred to me that they wouldn't want to fire a gun out here in the open where it could attract attention. Inside the factory had been different.

It gave me courage — a little, but nevertheless some courage.

I even stopped running and I walked the last few yards to the edge of the wharf. If I had to jump into the water and swim for it I'd need more breath than came from running at full tilt.

I had a bit of a sickener when I came to the edge of the wharf and looked down. That moonlight was good enough to let me see what lay below.

There wasn't any water.

Below, for a few feet out from the encrusted piles of the wharf was a sea of mud.

I didn't see myself jumping into that

slime and being able to struggle across into water deep enough to permit me to swim away. In fact there seemed no way of escape from that very high wharf.

I turned, standing in the moonlight between those twin rows of drums, and silently awaited my attackers.

The moonlight was full on their faces and they walked in advance of their squat shadows. They looked even bigger, even more hulking — even more threatening in that light. The stark white light of the moon seemed to give hollows to their eyes and under their broad cheekbones, and there was the shadow of their noses across their mouths so that they had the appearance of skulls as they came towards me.

Their pace slowed as they neared me, until they were moving at less than walking pace. They had strung out, as far as those rows of drums would permit, and they were closing in a flanking movement, which threatened me on all sides except my rear. And there was the biggest threat of all, of course — the drop into the glutinous mud below the wharf.

I was crouching, my fists bunched and swinging threateningly, and as they came near I growled the most savage threats I could lay tongue to. And it didn't stop them a bit. They came slowly, stealthily towards me, so that I didn't know from which side the attack would come first. I could hear their heavy breathing, because they too had felt the effects of that long chase in the darkness.

And I could see their eyes now, the little glints where moonlight reflected upon their hard, staring orbs. There was no mercy in them; only calculation.

And murder . . .

The ape on my right jumped in suddenly, swinging a massive fist at me. I slugged him, and I put every ounce of viciousness into that blow. He hit me and he hurt me, but my God he didn't hurt me half as much as I hurt him. I got him just where his ribs joined together under his chest — they call it the solar plexus — and it seemed that I went right up to my elbow into his guts, and he went down writhing, agony distorting that face as it reeled back away from me.

I swung round to face the others, and I was shouting:

'You s.o.b.s., I'll do that to the lot of you!'

But I didn't. They did it to me. They were too big and too many, and they came in all at once, their fists chopping, their feet kicking, and I didn't stand a chance at all. I fought back for a second or two, teetering on the edge of that wharf. It must have looked quite a sight, if there had been anyone there to see me fighting for my life in the bright moonlight on this south bank of the Horn.

Then their weight swept me into space. Or maybe I deliberately took a step over the edge to get away from those thumping fists and painful shoes that hacked at me.

I remember one of them gave me a final crashing blow on the right ear as I went into space, and it sent me whirling round and round in mid-air like a Catherine wheel.

It dazed me, too, but an instinct from my old days of combat training with airborne troops started my legs running, and it had the effect of bringing me fairly well upright, so that when I did land I came down on my feet.

I came down in a way that was more painful than I can describe. That wharf was a good fifty feet above the level of this mudbank upon which it was built. I landed soft but from that height it hurt all the same and it took what was left of the breath out of my body.

I felt the resistance as my legs dove into mud. Then the angle of my fall threw me face forward along the mudbank, and every bit of breath was squeezed out in that moment. I fought for air and it was agony as it came back into my tortured, suddenly-emptied lungs.

I was lying on the mud and almost completely submerged in it, looking down the rows of cross-braced supports of the landing stage. I was resting on my elbows with my forearms already buried in the mud. In fact that mud was nearly up to my shoulders and only my head was clear of its surface. Even at that my face had smacked into it and I could hardly see for the slime, which now dripped from my nose and chin and covered my face.

I got my breath back and I got my senses into some sort of order. But it did me no good. Because I realized I was stuck fast there and I couldn't move. More, I had the sense to know that if I did try to move my struggles, for certain, would slowly drag me under that mud and I would be suffocated.

Panting, I got my face round so that I could look upwards. I saw the edge of the wharf bright in the moonlight against the dark, velvety blue of a star-studded night sky. I saw four round things like nuts protruding over the edge of the wharf and I knew them to be the heads of the apes. As I looked I caught the quick murmur of their voices, as if they were in consultation with each other. And then all four heads vanished — and it brought me no reassurance.

I lay there, my cheek resting on the mud, still gasping and suffering from what I'd just gone through. Joe P. Heggy certainly had had a night!

And then my lassitude left me and I became frantic again in my desperation to escape. For I could hear sounds above — the sound of clanking metal — and I knew what it betokened.

Those boys were going to make sure of me. The boys were going to roll one of those massive drums over the edge of the wharf on top of me!

I groaned, and started to struggle, and got one arm out of the mud, but that only sent the rest of me a little deeper. So I stopped struggling and looked through the grime on my face, up towards the edge of the wharf again.

I saw a head appear and I thought: 'That's the sonovabitch who's directing operations. He's going to tell them where to drop the drum.' And I could hear that drum being trundled, with a low rumbling sound, across the wharf above me.

I didn't seem to have a chance. I was held in a strait-jacket of mud, a sitting duck for those marksmen with drums weighing eight hundred pounds apiece.

I gave in then. There wasn't anything else I could do. I recounted my past life and tried to think of all the good things I had done to my fellow men since I was a man myself. That seemed to take less than half a second, and then I began to contemplate my sins.

I'd only just begun when I saw something monstrous move before me.

I'd fallen almost at the foot of one of the mighty wooden supports to that wharf. It was encrusted with shells and barnacles, and just at this point there was a diagonal strut joined on to it — one of the cross-bracings that kept the staging rigid. My despairing eyes caught a movement in the cleft where brace joined support. Something was moving there, something of curious and yet familiar shape. It was within inches of my face, but I couldn't draw away from it.

And then my hand, the one that had been raised out of the mud, was gripped, and I have never known a force so powerful, certainly not in human agency.

I found myself being plucked out of that sucking mud-bath, and I suddenly realized that that monstrous thing I had seen was a foot of gigantic proportions. This arm with the giant's strength heaved and I came sliding out from that clinging mess, and it seemed that my arm was being torn from its socket in the process. I didn't complain.

For as I felt myself coming out of the mud something smacked down into it just where I had been, and a wave of mud came up my back and washed over my head.

I couldn't see any more and I didn't know what was happening. Then it seemed that many hands grasped me and lifted me off my feet, and I felt as though I were in the grip of giants, because I knew I was being lifted easily into the air and whisked away. And Joe P. Heggy is no lightweight.

I don't know what I thought being carried along like that. I don't even know whether I was thinking at all. I was blinded by mud in my eyes and darkness, and I had no strength left following that appalling drop into that breath-taking mud. I suppose if I thought at all I merely thought that I'd been picked up by Turkish troglodytes or their equivalent. For I could sense in some way that I was being taken rapidly underground.

Then my head ran into something that caught in my muddy hair and I could feel it was some sort of hessian, perhaps a curtain of sacking. At the same time I got the smell of wood-smoke in my nostrils, and I began to see through the mud over my eyes. I could see the leaping gleams of firelight.

I was put down then, and fairly gently, too. I lay where I was for a few seconds and then I groaned and rolled on to my back and dug the dirt out of my eyes.

When I could see I thought of the pep talks that our coach had given us in our darkest hours against Yale or the Navy in college football games, and I went over them to myself and that gave me strength enough to sit up and look around me.

There wasn't much to see at all. I was in some sort of recess, probably at the back of the wharf, high above the water line. A shelf had been dug into the rocky shore, and over the entrance to it hung that curtain of sackcloth. My guess is that that curtain was intended to prevent the firelight from being seen by water police travelling along the Horn in their launches. I looked at the troglodytes, and I found myself gazing upon barbarian folk.

There were about eight of them, crouched round the red, leaping fire, and they looked a savage, unkempt people. Their hair was long and coarse and matted so that it came down over eyes that gleamed redly in that firelight and never left my face. They were in rags, as ragged a bunch of men as I've ever seen. And they were without boots or shoes to their feet and their pants' legs were ragged up to their knees.

But they were men, mighty men. Men filled with a strength such as rarely comes to most of mankind. They weren't any bigger than the average man, but their muscles were mighty in every part of their limbs and body.

For I knew them at a glance. I had seen these troglodytes many a time before. They were some of the porters of Istanbul.

If you wish to have goods moved, even today in Istanbul, it is generally cheaper to have them carried on the backs and heads of men than it is to employ motor transport. Labour is that cheap in Turkey, even today. You see them struggling up the hillsides carrying fantastic weights, sometimes with a headrope to support mighty loads on their backs, other times staggering with the full weight upon their solid-looking skulls. There is a story that any one of these porters can lift a grand piano onto his head and carry it from Galata Bridge right up to the heights of Pera without once stopping to have a rest. It is probably exaggeration. Probably they do rest — for quite half a minute.

They work as men were never intended to work, straining their lives away in the heat of a Turkish summer, and I have pitied them always because in the end it would be more efficient to use a few horse-power, as we do in the States. And I know that the lives of these men must be short because no man can survive a youth spent in this killing occupation.

I sat up as strength came back to me, and I even tried to scrape the mud off my clothes. It wasn't successful and I gave up the attempt. The fierce-looking porters were watching me, probably not knowing what manner of man I was because of my mud disguise. For all they knew I might even be one of them.

Then I spoke, and though probably none of them spoke English they would recognize me for a foreigner immediately.

I said: 'Boys, I sure owe you a lot for what you just did for me. Let me get my breath back and we'll talk about throwing a party, shall we?'

The sound of my American voice seemed to fill them with suppressed excitement. I saw those troglodytes, their faces illuminated by the hot coals of that smouldering fire, turn and talk to each other in that quick succession of guttural sounds which is Turkish. And then one of them got up off his mighty haunches and came padding on work-calloused feet towards me.

He bent over me, and he wasn't fastidious in the least. He showed no revulsion at grabbing the slimy object that was Joe P. Heggy, and hoisting him roughly to his feet. I wouldn't have had the strength to resist even in my normal condition, because these were trained weightlifters and you don't stand much chance against the professional in any branch of life. I felt his huge hand dig into my pocket, and he came out immediately with my pocket-book.

He knew at once that he was in the money and he went back to the fireside and I saw the boys gather round excitedly to examine the contents of that wallet. It hadn't suffered at all in the mud-bath, unlike its owner, and the currency was readily identifiable. To me it didn't amount to much. Maybe the equivalent of a couple of hundred bucks in Turkish money and a few bits of paper representing change from visits to Greece and Cyprus and other territories. But to these ragged men it must have been wealth beyond their dreams.

I stood there, swaying, watching them, and I didn't give a damn even if they were robbing me. The hell, I would have given it to them for hoicking me out of that mud! I even said so.

I went a little uncertainly in amongst

them, and reached down for my pocket-book. The papers inside were valuable to me and of no use to the porters, so I wanted to take it.

But they got the wrong idea. They thought I was trying to get my money back, and one of them grabbed me by the wrist and did painful things to it and shoved me back against the rocky wall, and his face was savage and the glare in his eyes was murderous. These men lived such a hard life that a killing in order to give themselves a tiny, unaccustomed comfort would not trouble their consciences at all.

I knew he didn't understand me but I kept talking. I kept saying: 'Look, brother, I don't want that goddamned money. You can keep it. Dammit, I'll come back with a bucketful, if that's all you need. But I want those papers.'

And after a time I think those porters got the gist of what I was saying. The big, muscular troglodyte who had held me released his grip, and then, as is the way with their kind, he became suddenly friendly in the big expansive way of a schoolboy.

They held out my pocket-book and I took it, and then I looked towards the money and I waved my muddy hand in a way to suggest, the hell, I didn't want it, anyway!

That made us friends all round. They relaxed and laughed a lot and slapped me on my back, and I just wished then that they'd stopped at laughing. They made coffee in Turkish fashion in a tiny battered copper pan and though there was no sugar to go with it, it tasted good to me and I felt better after the drink. And then I went to one side because I felt that if I didn't rest I'd collapse, and I lay down on the bare rock and fell asleep.

When I awoke I was a corpse. I was neatly laid out with my hands folded across my stomach and I was entirely nude.

I was also so cold that for minutes I couldn't move my bruised limbs because of the chill in my muscles. The fire was out, and was just a mound of black ashes to my left. The curtain must have been drawn back because light came reflecting from the distant water and mirrored in moving patterns on the rough rock wall of this small hideout of these porters, probably too poor to pay for better lodgings.

I lay there and watched those moving, dappled sun patterns on the rough-hewn rock roof above me, and I thought that I was never going to move again

Added to my coldness was an intolerable stiffness that came from bruised and tired muscles. I'd been smacked around more than somewhat, then tossed fifty feet into mud, which was only soft when you tried to stand up in it. And that was enough for any man's body for quite some time, and now I was having to pay for the ill treatment.

But in the end the corpse moved. In the end I had to move, because I couldn't go on lying there. Anyway, with wakefulness had come the realization that a rocky bed isn't exactly comfortable to rest upon. I moved and got myself into a sitting position, though every muscle in my body seemed to creak with the effort.

And then, somehow, I got to my feet,

and stood swaying there while a dizziness passed over me.

I looked at myself and realized that my hands up to my forearms were black with encrusted mud. My hair was solid with dried mud, too, and I guessed that my face and neck were covered with the damned silt. I knew that I looked a sight, with my pretty, pink clean body and my muddied arms and head, but there wasn't a thing I could do about it.

I was sore, and I'm not meaning just physically, either.

I'd gone to sleep during the night with a feeling of confidence in those rough porter fellows. I felt they were friends and that no harm would come to me.

But in the night, when I was sleeping a sleep so deep that it came close unto unconsciousness, they'd stripped me of everything I had and had gone off, leaving me in my nudity.

It seemed a lousy trick to play on a man, especially after I had so willingly given them all the money I'd possessed. After all, I argued, my clothes wouldn't be worth a damn to them after the brawling I'd done in them the previous evening. They might at least have left me my rags, I kept growling.

Probably anger helped me to recover quicker than I'd expected. The hot blood came rushing into my veins as I thought of the doggone heels who had left me in this state.

I didn't wince now as I walked about, and the walking helped to free my muscles.

But swearing under my breath wasn't helping the situation at all. I felt singularly helpless. I mean, what does a fellow do when he finds himself stranded in the middle of a city — a foreign city at that — without any clothes? I shivered at the thought of finding my way out to a street. This low quarter of Istanbul wouldn't take to a naked foreigner suddenly appearing and being unable to explain why he went abroad in daylight without any clothes on. There'd be a lot of trouble about it, and in my mind's eye I pictured angry mobs coming to knock the hell out of the foreigner for offering insults to their womenfolk.

But even more I was afraid of what the boys would say if they had to come and bail me out for an indecent display of manhood here in Istanbul.

Someone giggled.

My head gawked round in an instant.

Two girls had come to the entrance where the sacking curtain had hung and were looking at me.

7

Lavinia Again

They were two young, broad-thewn young women, clearly of this strong, porter stock. They were what you'd dismiss as a peasant-type, though pleasant enough creatures because youth was still on their side.

Their hair was jet black and coarse and hung in disorder over their shoulders. They had broad solid faces that were brown in the manner of women who had to work in the sun; but they were rather jolly faces, especially now when they were laughing at me, and there were merry lights in their brown, good-tempered eyes.

They were barefooted, and like their menfolk, constant walking and working in bare feet had made them of unusual size. They would have created a sensation if they had gone into a 5th Avenue shoe shop and asked for the latest footwear.

And they wore one simple garment, a kind of Mother Hubbard such as the missionaries used to give out to Tahiti maidens in the old days. One look at those thin cotton dresses told you that that was all they wore.

They were giggling there and looking a bit bashful and coy, and they weren't making any move to come near me. But Joe P. Heggy wasn't abashed in the least. I've never seen what harm it does a man to be looked on by the other sex as I was then. And I didn't give a damn if I did look funny.

All I knew was that in those girls' hands were a pile of neatly-folded clothing. And if those weren't my pants on top, I was a bluenosed Hottentot. And my nose isn't blue.

I went quickly up to the girls, my hands outstretched, and they started to run away from me, so I stopped and hollered at them, because I didn't want to lose my pants a second time.

I stood there and saw them halt on the mud between the mighty, green-encrusted supports to the wharf overhead. There was water under the wharf now, as if the small tide which creeps into the Horn was at its fullest.

When they saw me beckoning impatiently towards them, they had a quick chatter together, laughing in some sort of feminine hysteria the while, and then slowly they came back into this small rocky cell that was home to their porter friends.

I reached out and grabbed my pants when they came near enough. I was so obviously concerned about getting into my clothes that the girls lost some of their feelings of uncertainty. While I got myself zipped up they chattered and squealed with laughter while they regarded me.

I said: 'Go on, gals, give yourselves a good laugh. Sure, I know I look a clown, like this, but I'm alive, aren't 1? So why should I worry?'

And quite truthfully I didn't seem to have a worry in the world just then. I'd survived the night and my fears in regard to my lost clothing had proved groundless. Relief came with the thought that I wouldn't have to make an exhibition of myself, and it flooded out any previous thoughts that had been tinged with acrimony.

I said: 'And you give the boys my thanks. It sure was mighty thoughtful of 'em to get my clothes washed and dried in time for me to use them today.'

They didn't understand a darned word I was saying, but you can't get yourself dressed under the very interested inspection of two sturdy and not uncomely females without saying something.

As I finished dressing I told them the show was over. I suppose they weren't used to seeing such soft, pink and white flesh such as we shirted individuals from the pampered West possess. I suppose the only men they knew were those mighty carthorses of creatures, with muscles like board and a skin like leather. They'd never seen a man like Joe P. Heggy, and they were marvelling at me, and I felt inclined to simper then, like some little girl who had got the eye of he-wolves upon her.

I felt smart when I was in my neatly-pressed, newly-cleaned suit. Even my wallet and keys and other pocket impedimenta had been replaced. It was only when I remembered that I was caked in mud all over my head and that my hands didn't look their usual hygienic whiteness, either, that some of the sense of smartness left me.

I said to the girls: 'Go on, gals, get me out of here.'

They got me all right. They turned and went clambering among the rocks under this huge high wharf, and I realized we were following a little pathway which gradually climbed up and round the end of the structure. We came out where some crazy, tumbledown ruins of houses started where the wharf ended. I found myself walking down a narrow cobbled alleyway that was almost white in the hot morning sun.

As soon as my feet were on the street, the two girls scurried away. I understood. There's a lot of the harem atmosphere about Turkey, in spite of the efforts to put an end to the old religious beliefs, and these girls didn't dare be seen in public with an infidel.

People came to their doors as I strolled

along — mostly women but with children and some old men among them, too. I looked into astonished, brown, wrinkled faces, and I quickly averted my eyes and walked with all the dignity I could muster. I tried, in fact, to give the impression that there was nothing an American liked better than to cake his hands and head in mud and then take a morning stroll in the sunshine.

It didn't kid the kids, however, and they came after me in their rags and bare feet, with their skulls shorn to the bone almost. And they shouted with delight, and said things that couldn't have been complimentary.

And then I came out in a square where there was a lot of traffic and I stopped all that traffic because excited people came running across to see me. I could only thank God I'd had my trousers brought back to me!

Fortunately a man with enterprise in charge of a taxi realized I had need of him, and he crashed his way through the crowd and held open the door of his big American limousine invitingly. I went inside so quickly, I nearly went through the far window. I gave the address of my hotel and we lurched away.

We roared majestically up towards the swank quarter of Pera. As we came up the steep, winding hill road under that Turkish sun which was already swelteringly hot, we overtook a column of porters on a removal job.

That's exactly what it was — a removal job.

Some of the men were carrying heavy, upholstered chairs upturned on their heads, and they were the luckiest. For another barelegged, ragged-trousered porter was staggering under a long, ornate, heavy ottoman. Yet another had a sideboard of early-Victorian design on his thin-shirted shoulders, and then came others bearing enormous bundles of bedding in which doubtless were wrapped family essentials such as pots and pans and other kitchen utensils.

I leaned from the big American-type taxi as we shot past them, intent on recognizing any of my late friends if it were possible. But they all looked alike

— they were all unshaven, ragged, barefooted, muscular men, sweating their hearts out under those intolerable burdens under that oppressive sun and up a hillside that made even my taxi driver have to change down.

We gave them our dust, and I settled back in my seat and I thought about the waste of human life in these countries.

I wasn't given long to ruminate and become philosophical, because all at once we were running with a smack of broad tyres along the cobbled street which led to my hotel — we were in the most crowded part of the city, and in danger of death from the clumsy, low-decker tramcars, which were a source of menace to every one of the fashionable shoppers along that congested street.

I was a sensation again when I reached my hotel. The taxi driver got alarmed when he saw me streak out from the cab without paying him, and he came after me. People on the sidewalk stared in astonishment when they saw a smartly-dressed man, muddied all over his head and hands, come rushing to where the revolving doors of the hotel were. But I was through the crowd before they had time to do more than look astonished.

I was inside that hotel and thumping the desk to get Benny's attention. Because Benny was back on duty again, and I was beginning to wonder if he ever went off.

Benny looked horrified when he saw the muddied apparition before him. He didn't recognize me until he heard my voice. And then he looked so sick, I knew that he had been told that Joe P. Heggy wasn't a man to worry about any more.

I glared through my mud at him, because there was nothing else I could do. And I rapped: 'Benny, I've got no money. Give this cab driver what I owe him, and a tip besides.'

And then I asked for my room key . . . and it wasn't there.

Benny was plainly puzzled, too, and when he said: 'Maybe you left it in your room,' I was inclined to agree with him. I couldn't remember handing it in when I went out with B.G. and little Lav the previous evening.

I went up to my room. At my call, the Turk who looked after the third floor shuffled forward in his heavy slippers and grinned at me through the scrub on his face. He fished out his bundle of keys. He opened the door. He was waiting for a tip. I waved him away, and said:

'Some other time, brother. Just now you've got more dough on you than I have.'

I closed the door in his smiling, supplicating face, and tramped into my apartment.

I saw a chair.

I saw some things on it.

They were women's things.

I didn't need to look closely at them to know what they were, either. For one awful moment I had a feeling that the Turk had let me into the wrong apartment, and then I spotted a familiar slipper under the bed — the slipper that had hammered the life out of that cockroach the previous evening in the bathroom. I knew I was at home then.

I looked at the bed. Someone was in it. I saw hair — just a little, touching the pillow.

I don't do things by halves, and I took a handful of bedclothes and I dragged them right back.

Someone sat up and screamed. It was Miss Dunkley.

Eighty-five per cent of Miss Dunkley was revealed by that sudden withdrawal of bedclothes. That other fifteen percent was covered by the briefest of slips. I stared at her, and I thought: 'My god, with a face like that . . . ' And then my eyes dropped a little and I began to change my mind. Miss Dunkley had a trim, shapely little torso when you got down to seeing it. And for a second I was seeing it. Her face first thing in the morning wasn't anything to get excited about, and I was left wondering where the youthfulness had gone that had begun to glow in her cheeks at Achmet's, the night before.

Then Lavinia scooped up the bed-clothes and pulled them up round her neck and looked at me as though I was the devil himself.

At which moment there was a knock on the door.

8

Sabotage

I let that knock go unattended. I was just realizing that my appearance must have been a shock to a late sleeper after the previous night's events. I mean it isn't every day that a spinster woman has the bedclothes dragged back by a man with the remains of a mudpack on his head.

I blinked at her, because she was the last person I had expected to find in Joe P. Heggy's bed.

But it was my bed and I felt entitled to gripe about it.

I said: 'For heaven's sake, Lav, what're you doing in there? Why aren't you in your own bed?'

She seemed relieved when she recognized my voice, but she didn't abate her grip on those tightly-held bedclothes at all. She sat huddled there, her eyes staring at me in horror. Then I heard her voice

156

whisper: 'Oh, my goodness, Mr. Heggy, what will you think of me?'

I started to strip off my jacket. I wanted to get out of this mud. So I told her I didn't have any thought about her at all, so she could take a vacation from holding onto those clothes. But I did ask again: 'For land's sake, don't you know your own bed by now?'

A flush came to those trembling cheeks, and her eyes grew a little moist. I heard her tremulous voice whisper: 'It was Mr. Gissenheim.'

I was taking off my shirt, but I stopped at that and turned on her: 'You mean B.G. stuck you in this room?' What was wrong with her own room in the same hotel?

She nodded. She was so awfully ashamed that she confessed to me before she knew what words were coming from her chaste lips.

'He — he put me in here, and said it was his room, and he would come in just as soon as he got himself a drink.'

Enlightenment dawned on me then. B.G. still Saving Himself Up for the Right

Woman, had played a low-down cunning trick on poor Lav. He'd ditched her neatly. He must have asked for my key and stuck her in my room, while he went and locked himself in his own apartment. No doubt he had gone to sleep quivering with fear, because of the threat to his chastity. And Lav, tired by an unusual night's dissipation, must have gone to sleep waiting for B.G. to come to her.

I said: 'Lav, you're a naughty girl, and you should be ashamed of yourself!'

She hung her head, the blush deepening on her cheeks, and I heard her say: 'I am!' And then she lifted her eyes to mine and they looked bewildered, and she said, her voice rising into a little wail: 'I don't know what's come over me since I came to this country! I — I think it's something in the atmosphere.'

She lifted her hand to push back a wisp of hair and she was trembling. Her eyes were big and wondering, and I could sense the emotions that gripped her.

'I must have been mad last night,' she whispered. Then her eyes lifted to mine and as quickly dropped away from them.

For I was shaking my finger at her and being very severe. I said: 'Come off it, Lav. You know darned well last night you went hunting for a man and you should be ashamed of yourself.'

I could tell her story right away. A little sex-starved spinster back in England, brought up to think what the neighbours would say and missing all the fun in consequence. Then, when it was almost too late, she had come, for her own reasons, to this distant, romantic country and the atmosphere had been like alcohol to her. She had recklessly tried to make up for lost time, here in Istanbul. She'd decided to have a fling before it was too late, and she'd suddenly gone with determination into it.

I thought: 'That B.G. . . . ' B.G. was not the kind of man she should have picked on. It was just her luck that she had picked on an inhibited guy who was no use to any woman. I told her so.

And then I asked: 'Why did you pick on B.G.?'

She whispered: 'I heard that all

Americans were — '

I nodded. I said, without bitterness: 'You're right — except for one man, B.G. And we like being that way, instead of you poor suppressed Britishers, who'd like to be like we are, only you don't dare.'

I couldn't stand that knocking on the door any longer, so I went across and opened up from the inside. Three men were standing in the corridor — Marty, Dwight and Tony Geratta. They were all spruced up and clean; and fresh-looking, and you wouldn't have believed they'd been in any drunken brawl the previous night.

When they saw me their faces registered horror. I said tiredly: 'Come on in. I'll tell you about this facial later.'

They came in. I didn't even mention Lavinia. But Dwight saw the feminine duds, and then he turned and saw the huddle under the bedclothes, for Lavinia had taken cover again.

Dwight said: 'Aren't we in the way, kind of?'

He jerked his head towards the bed. I

was getting out of my pants. I said: 'The hell, no, that's not mine — that's B.G.'s.'

I slung my pants across a chair and gave Lavinia's virginal underwear a treat. The boys knew by the way I talked that I wasn't stringing them, and they went to the bed to have a look. Dwight got roguish, and started saying bitty-witty things, such as: 'Peep-bo, let uncle see your bright blue peepers.'

Uncle was disappointed. Lavinia refused to rise to the blandishment.

I got under the shower. I could see what was going on when I stuck my head round the corner, but Lavinia's modest eyes couldn't have been shocked by sight of my undressed form.

They got the clothes back a bit and saw her frightened little face underneath, and they recognized it, and then they all sat on the bed and talked to her. They were getting one hellofa kick out of it, and they were doing a lot of finger wagging and being reproving and poor little Lavinia went through hell. She'd never had so many men around her bedside before.

From the shower I gave them a brief explanation. 'B.G. stood her down. He's still Saving Himself Up for the Right Woman, I guess, and Lav isn't it. So he ditched her in my bedroom, saying it was his.'

Marty looked at the other boys, and said: 'That was an ungentlemanly thing for B.G. to do. He's a slob, Lav. We'll take him apart for treating you like this.' He looked at his companions, virtuously. 'We wouldn't ever do a thing like that, now would we, boys?'

There was an embarrassing hesitation, as the boys looked upon that not-too-young, early-morning face of an ageing woman. Before they had time to lie, I growled through the streaming mud that was coming out of my hair: 'If you'd seen what I'd seen, you wouldn't be so slow in agreeing with Marty, boys.'

I got out of the shower. The curtain still protected Lavinia's maidenly eyes from sight of my wet torso. I said, calling through it: 'What brought you boys up here so early? And how did you know I was back at the hotel?'

Dwight wandered over. He had had all the fun he wanted out of Lavinia. He leaned against the wall and lit himself a cigarette — one of mine. He said: 'The hell, Joe, we got kind of worried about you last night. We even went and saw the police when you didn't turn up, and I guess they're combing the town for you right now.'

But then Marty came pushing up, remembering.

'Quit beefing, Dwight,' he said quickly. 'This — ' his hand swept round to indicate the terrified Lavinia huddling back among the bedclothes again — 'took our minds off the reason for our visit to your apartment, Joe.'

I stopped rubbing my hair. I felt apprehensive. 'Come on, out with it. What happened in the night?' As if enough hadn't happened to Joe P. Heggy!

Marty said: 'A mob got itself loose on our equipment, and they've torn it apart. It's not working today and Gorby isn't sure whether he can get it working in weeks.'

I didn't think of anything except that

163

equipment after that. I strode out, still wet from the shower, and started to get into another suit. I didn't even look to see if Lavinia was taking a peek at me. My job with Gissenheim's was just beginning.

Trouble had broken out, and when I wasn't nurse-maiding B.G., I was the firm's trouble-buster.

I said, as I got into a shirt: 'What happened? Tell me all you know.'

We were on a big job, a few miles out of Istanbul. It was all part of United Nations' work of course — just another airfield being laid down. The only trouble was that this airfield was to have one of those super-long runways, and there was a super-high hill in the way just where they didn't want it, and then a ditch the size of the Pentagon sitting right next to that hill.

Gissenheim's had got the contract to dig out that hill and level it, and in the process fill in that gulch.

It was a mighty job, but it wasn't exceptional for Gissenheim's. We brought in all our dirt-shifters from Beirut, where we'd been doing other work, and we'd been tearing into that hill for a few days.

We had the finest equipment in the world for the job — I'll say that of Gissenheim's. Everything was mechanical, and things stabbed into that hillside and clawed at it and gouged out tons of earth at a time and slung it all backward on to moving belts, which took it to where it was wanted. It was such a spectacle, that daily thousands of people tramped out to watch the mighty Gissenheim earth-shifters at work.

Now I was being told that the equipment had been sabotaged.

Dwight said: 'I've been out and seen it, Joe. I spoke with some of the men who were guarding the place during the night. They said they had a terrific fight with hundreds of attackers who suddenly, quite silently, sprang out at them. My guess is there weren't more than a dozen, and those watchmen got the hell out of it when they realized there was trouble coming up.

'The saboteurs, whoever they were, did things I wouldn't have believed possible.

They tossed every conveyor onto its side — though that didn't do them any harm; they can soon be put into position again. But they went to work on the cutters and the grabbers and they smashed up everything they could smash. Gorby is inclined to be pessimistic because he's got a hangover, but he sure has got a job ahead of him, and I don't know whether we carry enough spares.'

I got on my jacket and began to lace up my shoes.

I said: 'We'll fly spares in from the States rather than fall behind on this job. You keep your fingers crossed, Dwight — Gorby moans, but he works miracles.' I stood up and hitched a tie around my neck. I said: 'Let's have your suspicions — now.'

Marty shrugged. He said: 'It could be political.'

It was my turn to shrug. 'Could be,' I agreed.

Dwight said: 'We bust a few friendships when we got this contract. Could be some rivals don't want us to make a shine on this job.'

I was walking towards the door. I agreed again.

'Could be.' We'd tendered in the face of severe competition, and some rivals — American outfits — hadn't risen to their size by kid-glove methods. Trouble could have come from them, easily.

I looked at Tony Geratta, handsome and smiling. He was a good boy, that Tony. I said: 'You got any theories to contribute?'

Tony shook his head.

I said: 'So it seems we're reduced to two.' I was suddenly reminded of Lav, huddled in my bed.

I halted and looked at her and caught a frantic eye peering at me between hair and blanket. I was kind. I said: 'We'll get that big slob, B.G., and send him up to you, Lav.'

She came out of her blankets at that, terror gripping her. She exclaimed with horror: 'Oh, please, Mr. Heggy, don't do that: I — I don't ever want to see him again!'

I inclined my head. I said: 'I never did see what you saw in that guy. Except that he was American.'

She whispered miserably: 'I'll go as soon as you've gone, Mr. Heggy. I'm sorry I used your bed. I didn't know . . . '

I said kindly: 'That's all right. Any time I'm not using it, you climb in.'

Which was perhaps a departure from the usual Heggy code of gallantry.

We went out. The elevator wasn't working again.

We walked down. When I got to the foyer I saw something magnificent walking towards me.

And she was magnificent.

It was Marie Konti. And it wasn't the bogus Marie Konti — the girl who had lured me into Room 102 yesterday.

This was the real Marie Konti. I knew it at once.

For this girl's face was that face that I had looked down upon from my bedroom window — it was the face I had seen in that intense moonlight the previous evening.

It was the face of the girl who had been abducted by those apes . . .

She came straight up to me, and her

168

cheeks were burning, and she said: 'Are you Mr. Heggy?'

I nodded.

She exclaimed loudly, angrily: 'Then will you please stop making a nuisance of yourself!'

9

Kidnapped Again

That hotel foyer was pretty small; for it had been designed before the era of air transport and travel on an international scale. And all at once it seemed to be the most crowded place in Istanbul. More than that, it seemed the most zany.

Because right at that moment B.G. decided to join us and immediately the boys set onto him.

Perhaps they hadn't noticed the way in which Marie Konti had addressed me — or perhaps it was just their idea of adding to the jollity of the moment. They were three gents of distorted humour, those buddies of mine.

Behind Marie Konti I was suddenly aware of a sleek man. He was a Turk in the modern style. Obviously an intelligent man, and as sharp as they're made. Rather big, just going fleshy, and so dapper we knew at once that he did his shopping in Rome or Paris.

I saw this rube, and I said to myself, right away: 'Watch your mouth, fellow. This is a lawyer.'

And I was right.

But I also saw Benny's face over the reception desk and if I'd ever seen malicious triumph in my life, it was on Benny's mug. I thought: 'You sonovabitch, you've been telephoning again!'

And I noticed someone else, in the background behind this sleek, confident lawyer man . . .

I heard that lawyer man speaking, but I didn't hear what he was saying. I was looking into that lovely face of Marie Konti's. I was noticing the flush that made her look so attractive, and the shining brightness of her eyes.

I was also noticing that those shining bright eyes looked keyed up to the point of desperation, and I tucked that thought into my brain to be looked at later. Marie Konti plainly was in a dither.

I didn't hear what that lawyer man was saying, because Marty and the boys were taking the pants off their employer. They were giving him hell in public, and they were enjoying it.

There was Marty, trumpeting indignantly: 'You should be ashamed of yourself. I never knew a man like you. You get a girl crazy over you and then you stand her up.'

Dwight shouted cheerfully: 'You're a heel!'

And Frankie put in some good work with: 'She'll sue you. Goddammit, she ought to sue you. This'll set you back a quarter of a million.' And at that B.G. winced, because he knew what quarter of a million the boys were referring to. It was what an indiscretion of his could have cost the firm but for their resource and loyalty to Gissenheim's.

He started to shout at them, his eyes darting frantically everywhere behind his glasses, appalled to find himself the centre of a scene in a public place. He was bleating: 'I didn't ask her to chase me. I don't care if some sex-starved female does get a yen for me. I'm not interested in women.'

Marty spread his hands and looked around the hotel. He said: 'Casanova says he's not interested in women. He must have had a bad night.'

And Frankie called out: 'Mebbe he's got a conscience.' And Dwight's comment was a laconic, 'Mebbe.'

I concentrated on the lawyer man while B.G. went around bleating furiously: 'You're tearing my character to shreds. You know damn' well I never gave that dame any encouragement. There ought to be a law to protect men against women like her.'

Now the lawyer man was beginning to register. He was saying: 'Mr. Heggy, my client informs me you reported to the police that she had been abducted from this hotel last night. That news has caused distress among her friends. My client demands a full and proper explanation and, failing that, I'm afraid this matter will have to go before a Turkish court.'

My eyes I'm sure were glinting hard at that sleek, well-dressed lawyer. I'll bet my face looked as inviting as the steel jaws of a Gissenheim mountain grabber right then. I said: 'Listen, pansy, I saw what I saw.' My eyes flickered to that lovely girl who seemed to be watching me in such distress and agony, and yet was shrinking away from me. I said, my voice grating: 'I saw so much of you, sweetheart, I could describe you perfectly.' But I didn't. My eyes were looking beyond the lawyer man at another man who had just entered the foyer. This newcomer was my police shadow of the night before.

Marie Konti was almost crying, as if she didn't want this scene in public and was trying hard to make me believe her story. She called, with that rising note that Europeans get when they're excited:

'I never left my apartment all last night, I was out when the police came, but I reported to them by telephone immediately afterwards.'

I looked at the tall young man standing alongside my shadow. That tall young man was the Turkish police officer. He was standing silently there, listening intently, but when I looked at him he gave a little nod as if to confirm what Marie Konti was saying.

My eyes fell to her hands. She was carrying a room key to which was attached a large brass number plate. I could see the number on it and it was 102.

I said: 'You can do what the hell you like. My story stays the same as it was. And I'll add to it. There was another dame passing off as Marie Konti when I went up to her room last night. She had boyfriends, too, and they were playful. They tried to drop me on my head down an empty elevator shaft, and then they tried to rough me up in the Galata area.

'They even used a gun on me, when they thought it was safe.' I was speaking now for the benefit of that Turkish police officer, and everybody there knew it.

'I've been knocked around by four big apes, and I'm sore about it. Let me tell you that I'm sticking to my story, and if I get the chance I'll do things to those apes that will be a shame!'

Joe P. Heggy's blood was up. This lovely girl was lying, and that lawyer man knew she was lying, and they were trying to make me look a fool. I wasn't having any of it, and I was putting out a challenge to them deliberately to come and have another smack at Joe P. Heggy.

For I was beginning to think of a plan to do unto those others what they wanted to do to Joe P. Heggy. I was forgetting that I am normally a nervous man.

The lawyer-man got very brusque and he said: 'Very well, if that's your attitude, I have no alternative but to go to the Courts, and complain about your behaviour.'

I had a feeling then that he said it significantly, but it didn't impinge for the moment. I just nodded and started to push my way past them, because I was on a job of trouble-busting and private interests came second to those that gave me my paycheck.

I couldn't resist it, however. As I went past the attractive Marie Konti I said: 'Honey, any time you want a big brother, come and weep on my shoulder.'

She said something. It was a whisper. I walked past as if I hadn't heard, as if she hadn't said anything. B.G. and the boys, still yapping at him, came up behind me.

The big young police officer turned and went through the doors ahead of me. There was a police car alongside the sidewalk. B.G. and the others started to go round the alley where taxis usually parked, but I dallied to have words with the police officer.

I looked at my shadow and said: 'Brother, I didn't ditch you purposely. Things just happened. I'd have given a million to have had you tailing me later last evening.'

I don't think he believed me. I think under that impassive countenance he felt sore because I had apparently tricked him, and he had fallen down on a job. I had a feeling it wasn't too good to fall down on a job in the police force of Istanbul.

The big young police officer was slapping his gloves into his empty palm — a characteristic habit of the man. He said nothing, but his eyes were smiling invitingly, suggesting that I opened up to him.

I stood in the sunshine on that sidewalk, my head bent, and I brooded for a second, and then I lifted my eyes to his and said: 'How much do you know of Von Papen?'

My question startled the police officer. He repeated: 'Von Papen?'

I nodded: 'Yeah, I know a bit about him. He was Hitler's ambassador here in Turkey around 1943, wasn't he?'

The police officer nodded. The smile had left his face and he seemed to be watching me narrowly.

I said: 'What else can you tell me about Von Papen?'

The police officer was nonplussed. Again his shoulders shrugged, and he said; 'I don't know much about him. He didn't last long.' His eyes seemed to be thinking back. 'He didn't approve of foreigners,' the handsome, well-groomed young officer said abruptly, and then he explained a little more fully. 'He caused a law to be passed by the Turkish government at the time, a law which aroused a lot of interest throughout the world, I remember.'

I began to feel a little excited, as if I felt that the dawn of revelation was at hand. I said: 'Go on!' — quickly.

'That law said that any foreign nationals resident in Turkey lost all rights of return if they left the country even for the shortest of periods.'

I began to nod. I remembered that law. It was really anti-Semitic, aimed at Jews, principally, resident in Turkey, in accordance with Hitler's racial theories.

But I couldn't for the life of me see how this tied up with the abduction of a pretty girl — and her later reappearance.

For those were the two words that Marie Konti had whispered to me when I passed her just then — 'Von Papen.' That's what she'd said.

I shook my head.

That husky young police officer was trying to smile again. But his eyes weren't smiling. They were searching my face, trying to read through the riddle. He asked: 'I do not understand. What is this talk of Von Papen? What has Von Papen got to do with — '

He shrugged. He didn't need to enlarge upon this complex and mysterious affair.

I sighed, and it was a sigh so long it

must have been a world's record. But I was a weary, puzzled man. I told him: 'Damned if I know,' and then I changed the conversation. 'Now, you tell me, who was that gink with Marie Konti?' I changed the conversation because I didn't want him to know those were the two words uttered to me by Marie Konti.

The traffic went noisily by. People thronged the sidewalks, there was the babble of many tongues, and I saw faces that belonged to every continent in the world.

And yet, in the midst of all this almost-cheerful gaiety, I was standing there brooding, near to being disconsolate, so that it was only distantly and with half my mind that I heard that young Turk say, noncommittally: 'He is a big lawyer. He is the most powerful lawyer in the country, because he is also one of its most powerful men.'

I came out of my reverie then. 'You mean he's a politician?'

The officer nodded. He had his hand on the handle of the police car awaiting him. I think he didn't wish to be seen in too close a conversation with me after Marie Konti had appeared to discredit my statement.

And yet I knew without being told that this smart young officer was still on my side, and that meant that he believed my story. 'He's in the government, and a most powerful man.' I knew he was warning me to watch my step and I was grateful to him. 'His name is — '

It seemed to me that the officer gave a strangulated cough. I said: 'Pardon?'

He told me that that was the lawyer's name. I waved a paw. 'He can keep it,' I said. 'I'll go on thinking of him as the lawyer-man.' I brooded a second, and then changed my mind. 'Nope. From now on I'll call him a poisonous politician,' I said deliberately, 'Because he's all that, and you know it, brother!'

The Turkish officer nodded politely and got into his car. Through the open window he smiled at me and said, so confidently: 'Mr. Heggy, I'm leaving it to you to solve this case for me. I'm pretty sure they'll come after you again!'

So I said: 'This time, then, forget about

a police tail, will you?' Because my blood was up. I wanted to handle these murderous thugs in my own way. After all, wasn't my profession breaking down trouble when it appeared?

He nodded. 'As you wish,' he said. And that seemed to me to be a compliment. As if the police officer felt that I could hold my own even against powerful thugs.

The police car slid off. The boys, still going vigorously for a bewildered and unhappy B.G., got into a taxi round the alleyway. I told 'em to go ahead, I'd follow in another cab.

They didn't understand it, but I got short with them and they must have realized I was up to something, for Marty nodded and gave the word to the driver and the taxi went out into the main street with its horn screaming in true Istanbul fashion.

I went to the next taxi in the rank. The driver looked the kind of man I wanted — young, and with the light of adventure in his eyes. I took out a handful of kurus. That passes for money in Turkey. I shoved it into that astonished driver's hand, and it was probably more than he could earn with his cab in a fortnight.

I said: 'You do as I tell you and there's more kurus waiting for you at the end of this trip.'

He didn't understand, but he kept smiling quickly at me and nodding vigorously, and I knew it would be all right. I climbed in behind him. And the way he looked at me he must have thought I wanted to run somebody. And he was willing!

I got the window open behind him and put my hand on his shoulder. I told him: 'Go left, brother,' and I jerked my head to indicate the way I wanted. I was on my knees behind him now, but I was controlling him with my grip on his shoulder. That grip kept him down to a crawl, and he turned left and came slowly up into the position vacated by the police car.

A group was standing on the edge of the sidewalk. There was that big, sleek, politician-lawyer, talking to a fawning, uneasy-smiling Benny, and just to one side of them stood lovely Marie Konti.

Benny started to come along the sidewalk quickly, and I knew he was running round to get a taxi for the big boss. For I felt sure in my mind that this big huckster was the big boy behind all this skulduggery.

I stooped so that Benny didn't see me, and he passed on to the rank. I had one hand on the taxi driver's shoulder now, and the other on the door-handle. I lifted my eyes just above the level of the door frame, and right there before me was Marie Konti. The huckster was looking after Benny, for one second his attention diverted from the girl.

I let the door swing open, and I reached out and grabbed a wrist that was slim and smooth and soft, and I pulled, and Marie Konti came falling into the taxi on top of me. I had that door closed quicker than it takes to say it. And then that taxi driver earned his money, because he had seen what had happened, and he didn't wait for orders but put his foot hard on the accelerator and went up the hill like greased lightning. I don't think the huckster even realized that Marie

Konti had been snatched from underneath his nose into that receding taxi. She had been abducted a second time successfully — and by me this time!

For a few seconds I didn't get up, in case there were people watching the car who might recognize the kidnapper. We lay together in the well of the car, and Marie Konti didn't move out of my arms, either.

When I felt the car beginning to turn, I thought it was time to get up, and I pulled myself on to the broad, back seat. A glance through the window told me that we weren't, so far, anyway, being pursued. I looked down at Marie Konti. She was still lying there, and she was looking up at me with an unfathomable expression in her eyes.

She wasn't afraid of me, though. I felt glad about that.

I lifted her and helped her into the seat beside me. Then I leaned forward and told the driver to go out to the new airfield, and then I concentrated on the girl.

I offered a cigarette, but she shook her

head. She was sitting quietly by my side, smoothing her thin-silk, beflowered dress, which looked so clean and attractive upon her. She was watching me all the time, as if trying to understand what was in my mind — and failing all the time.

I said to her: 'You didn't mind being snatched away from — him?' I jerked my head back towards the hotel.

She shook her head.

I said, gently: 'You look like a girl wanting help. Can I help you?'

At that her eyes turned away, and I thought she was going to weep, and I don't like girls to get lachrymose. Then, thank goodness, she put aside her feminine tears, and said: 'I need someone to help me, but I don't know how anyone can.'

I came out with the usual gambit: 'Maybe if you told me about it . . . '

But she shook her head again, and she wouldn't talk, beyond saying: 'I want to keep away from that man for a while. He — he terrifies me!'

Well, just then we came out on to the

shambles that was the Gissenheim project.

Whoever had wrecked the equipment had done it pretty thoroughly. It looked to me as if a giant had been turned loose, to create the havoc that I saw.

The construction of an airfield is, in any event, always a scene of desolation. For as far as the eye could see on this low-lying dreary north coast of the Sea of Marmora, dirt had been grouted out, leaving the ugly grey-yellow under-soil exposed. The whole was crisscrossed with the deep ruts from transporter trucks, and the biting treads of caterpillar equipment.

But I saw more than that, because that desolation was familiar to me. I saw that the long roller-conveyors had been overturned and the belts ripped off. I saw the damage apparent on bulldozers, grabbers, grouters and cutters, and all the usual equipment required for a big Gissenheim project. It looked as if men had gone round with iron bars and smashed everything that could be smashed.

There were several little groups of people standing among that clustered mass of silent machinery, and I got the driver to take us over to where I could see Gorby Tuhlman, with his mobile work-shop. Marty was with him, but none of the other boys.

Marty looked interested in the girl in the back of the car when I got out. He jerked his head without saying a word. I said, laconically: 'I won second prize in a radio contest.' Marty looked interested. He said: 'What was first prize? A harem?'

Gorby looked up at me from a workbench scattered with ruins. His face was sour, the face of a man who has seen vandalism among things sacred to him. For these mighty muck-grabbers were like children to Gorby.

I said: 'How are things going, Gorby?'

He was savage. He said: 'Nearly the only thing they missed was the power-grab. I reckon they couldn't get up into the cabin to do any damage.' I looked round at all the other machinery. Ten million bucks' worth. 'It's all out of action?'

'It's all out of action,' Gorby nodded. For a moment he worked savagely with a box-key, adjusting something. He had some Turkish assistants at work, but they didn't seem to be getting on with the job very well. That was probably because we were short of spares on the scale required, and they weren't sufficiently well-trained to be able to improvise. Gorby said, toughly: 'But I'll have half this equipment going before tonight. By God, if I have to work my fingers down to the elbows, I'll have the cutters going, anyway!'

That was something. If the cutters could still go riving into the low, rounded hill that had to be cleared, we could at least keep somewhere close to schedule. Gorby was saying: 'I'm fixing floods all over the place. We'll have to take away the spoil on a three-shift system after this. The cutters can get the muck back, but until the conveyors are moving up into the hoppers we can't get it into the trucks.'

I nearly said: 'How about manual loading?' But fortunately I stopped. To Gorby, work done by hand was anachronistic in this age of mechanisation. There'd been tenders for this contract by local contractors who would have used gangs of labourers to transport muck in baskets on their heads. To employ such labour, even for a short while, would, to Gorby, be a confession that his beloved equipment wasn't up to the job, that there was something in those laborious, old-fashioned techniques after all.

So I said nothing, because Gorby looked as if he could use that spanner on anyone who crossed him, right then.

Dwight came up then. He'd been to cable to Detroit for a list of spares to be sent out by first possible plane. He was looking a bit grim. Evidently the list was a long one. He said to me, toughly: 'This is your meat from now on, you know, Joe.'

I nodded.

He went on: 'What guarantee have we that this won't happen again? If we lose more time, there's that forfeiture clause to reckon with if the job lags beyond the scheduled date.'

We knew what that meant. For every day that we had to work on this project beyond a certain date, Gissenheim's would have to forfeit a cool ten thousand bucks. A week behind schedule could take all the gilt off the gingerbread, in fact, quite apart from doing the firm's reputation an appalling amount of harm.

I said grimly to Dwight: 'Don't you worry about the future, brother. I started making plans an hour back.'

Dwight grinned at the big taxi sitting in our midst, with that lovely girl reclining in the deep upholstery.

He said: 'I figured you'd got your mind on other plans.'

I didn't answer that. For one thing I could see she was terrified out of her wits, just having to sit there in that taxi, not knowing what was ahead for her. I knew, as I watched her nervous little gestures, and the way her eyes went quickly from place to place, apprehensively, that she had had a bad twelve hours of it.

Marty lounged up, his red hair tousled, as if he had been helping with the repair work himself. He said: 'We're fixing the conveyor belts. But it means stripping them down and re-erecting them all over again. That's a couple of days' job before we can get them into operation and the trucks start moving with the spoil.'

Dwight jerked out a cigarette and then tossed the packet over to us. 'I was just telling Joe to watch out because whoever did this might like to give an encore.' Dwight took my proffered light, and then jerked his head towards a distant bunch of cheerful Turkish labourers. 'These watchmen we've got here aren't worth a damn.'

Marty nodded. 'I'm with you there, Dwight,' he said. 'They told me a good yarn about how they fought against the attackers last night, but my guess is they got the hell out of it the moment they saw there was trouble coming. I reckon they figure they don't get paid enough to have their faces knocked about.'

Dwight turned to me. 'You got that all figured in your plans?'

I said: 'I've got it all figured.' And then I said, toughly: 'I only hope to God they do make another attempt on Gissenheim's stuff.' I had plans, and they weren't nice ones for the saboteurs.

And then I told them they didn't need me any longer. I said I was clearing off for the day, because my work began after dark. They all looked at me then, and they all looked at the girl, and then they made cracks about my statement, and I realized it had been carelessly-chosen and invited their humour.

B.G. came over, and asked me for a lift back into town if I was going in with my taxi. I wouldn't take him all the way, because I didn't want to go anywhere near Pera where I might be recognized. I had a feeling that that lawyer-man would connect me in time with Marie Konti's disappearance and would be jumping in top gear to do something about it.

I'd got around to the significance of his statement in the foyer, finally. I'd remembered that if a serious charge is brought against a foreign national in Turkey, the foreigner is usually invited to clear out of the country pretty quickly in order to save a lot of bother. In other words, if that highly-placed politician wanted to, he could, in effect, get me deported by threatening civil court proceedings against me. And I knew that was just what he wanted — my abrupt deportation.

I dropped B.G. at a place where he could quickly expect to pick up a taxi. He didn't like being out in that hot sunshine on the construction job, and he wanted to get back to the hotel. His excuse was that he wanted to cable a full report to the Detroit office, but my guess was that he wanted to get his fat bulk on a bed and doze through the mid-day heat.

I had other plans, much more pleasant. We drove down to the harbour, where I paid off that taxi driver, who became my friend for life. Marie Konti walked passively when I took her onto a steamer. She didn't have any enthusiasm for anything, but she didn't want to leave me. Wherever I took her seemed good enough for her. I knew the kid was scared stiff of things happening to her, and I suppose she felt that I could protect and defend her.

We took a steamer out to one of the lovely islands in the Sea of Marmora. It was the largest, Buyukada.

When we came ashore at sunlit

Prinkipol, the largest town on the island, she seemed to throw off some of her fears, and there was a greater liveliness to her step, and she even smiled at me quickly when she caught my eye.

I took her by the arm, and she didn't resist, and we went across and got one of the open horse-drawn carriages, and I told the old driver to take us to the bathing station. I felt that the safest place for that girl that day would be in the anonymity of a crowded bathing beach. Somehow you can never recognize anybody among a throng of undressed people. Besides, I wanted to get her into a state of mind when she would tell me of her own free will what was back of this mystery. I had a feeling that if I began to question her, she would shut up like a clam, and then I wouldn't know and wouldn't be able to help her.

10

Interlude

It turned out much as I planned. I was nice to the girl, and I didn't ask her any questions, and in time she began to feel obliged to open up.

I got towels and swim suits and hired a 'family' cabin. We changed in turn and then went and lay in the hot sun under the shade of some tall eucalyptus trees. The sea was within yards of our feet, gently lapping; the sky was a glorious blue, and the atmosphere heavenly. Everywhere around us were bathers and people lying in the sun, but there was a soporific quality about that afternoon which made them restrained in any merriment, so that there were few sounds, and they seemed to drift lazily and acceptably to our drowsy ears.

We had iced drinks brought to us, and later we went to a beach cafe and had salads and coffee and lovely Turkish ice-cakes. Then we went for a stroll along the water's edge as the sun declined and a gentle coolness came to temper the heat of the day. Our feet splashed in the warm shallows. I held her hand clasped in mine, and she leaned against me and I could feel the warmth of her arm against my own. When we were well away from the bathers, among some rocks which came to form a spit out to sea, she sat down, and I sprawled myself at her feet. She was framed against the glorious blue of that Marmora sky — her gleaming coils of black, wavy hair reflected the brilliant sunshine, and the warmth of the day had brought a flush to her lovely face, and her eyes were suddenly bright and eager and hopeful. She was looking at me, and those eyes were brimming with friendliness — with more than friendliness, I began to think.

Suddenly she began to talk to me, and I was silent because I had waited for this. She said: 'I must tell you about this affair. I'm in terrible trouble, and I don't know how to escape from it. Worse than that,

I'm afraid trouble might come to other people — to my parents in Ankara.

'I'm sorry that I had to lie to you in the hotel foyer this morning. But I had no alternative.' Her head shook desperately, as if she were recalling the frustration of that moment, and the embarrassing scene that had followed it, when all eyes became centred upon Joe P. Heggy and herself.

'That lawyer-man, as you call him, has a hold on me. He can blackmail me and my parents and I cannot do anything about it if I wish to remain in Turkey.'

I looked up at her at that, but still kept silent, and she continued and it seemed that her confidence in me grew so that her speech became less halting and more eager in her efforts to explain things.

'You see, it all started when Von Papen became Hitler's ambassador to Turkey in 1943.'

I nodded. I knew what that connoted.

I found myself speaking then. 'It's something to do with your leaving this country? You're not a Turkish national?'

She shook her head, and her hair came across her bare, rounded shoulders and

198

emphasised their soft whiteness.

'My family have lived in Turkey for generations. My father is a prosperous merchant in Ankara, with big trade connections with Italy.

'Before the Von Papen law, as we still call it, was passed, he used to go regularly to Italy on business, and sometimes he would take his family with him. But now he is in this position, that he dare not go to Italy because if he leaves this country he, an Italian subject still, for all his long residence in Turkey, will be refused right of re-entry.'

Her shoulders shrugged helplessly. 'We like Turkey. We'd like to remain here. And besides, we have a fine business in this country, so we don't want to be refused the right to live and work here. However, there was nothing we could do about it, and my father hasn't been to Italy for more than ten years, though at times his business really does require him to go there.

'But I went there early this year. I found that if you put a bribe in the right place it was possible to have your passport manipulated so that it doesn't show any exit declaration. It's expensive, but this year it became necessary for me to go to Italy. My sister is married and lives there, and she was very ill. So we paid the bribe, and I flew to Italy. It worked beautifully, and seemed worth the money, because there was no trouble at all when I returned to Istanbul.'

Her eyes looked beyond me, out to the distant rolling waves of the sea. There was pain and worry returning to them now. 'The trouble began a few weeks after I returned. A man came to me and said it was a mistake — that I should have paid twice what I had paid for that passport manipulation. I told him that there was no mistake, and I refused to pay the money.'

I stirred. 'Good for you, baby. That's the way to treat blackmailers.'

She shook her head. 'It wasn't good for me. I had to pay him in the end, because one day he came with photographs, and those photographs showed me getting onto an aeroplane, they showed me walking the streets of Rome, and they showed my passport in the hands of the Immigration Officer at Rome airport.'

My eyes lifted and met those brown ones. They were frantic again as she recalled the helplessness of her situation.

She went on: 'It was no good fighting against the blackmailers. My father had to pay them, and, go on paying them. He wanted his daughter with him here in Turkey, and when they threatened to turn those photographs over to the Turkish Immigration Department, he knew they would keep their threat.'

She shrugged. 'He kept on paying them, and for six months he has never been free from their demands. Now we realize that the risks they took to get my passport manipulated was only in order to put me in a position to be black-mailed.'

Now she looked at me, and her hands seemed to wring with the panic and concern that gripped her. 'Oh, God, what can I do?'

I said: 'But you did finally refuse their demands?'

'I did.' She nodded. 'Finally, I decided I

couldn't see my father bled in the way they were bleeding him. So I thought that if I just disappeared it would end their hold on my father. I intended to return when it seemed safe to do so. I came to Istanbul, intending to hide out somewhere, but they were smart, and almost the moment I arrived at this hotel they were here to meet me. They came to my room, and they told me not to try to go into hiding — they ordered me to go back to my father, so that they could resume their blackmailing. I told them I wasn't going back, that I was going to hide myself where they would never find me.'

The girl shivered. 'I went to bed early that night, filled with this resolve next day to go into hiding. Soon after I got to bed I saw the door opening, and then two big men came rushing into my room. One of them said: 'You're coming with us. Don't shout, because that'll be so much the worse for you. If you do the police will just get to know you have forfeited your residential qualification in Istanbul.' They dragged me into the elevator, which the hotel clerk operated. Then they took me outside into a car — '

I nodded. 'That's where I came in.' I was remembering that scene, the first time I had seen Marie Konti. And I was remembering her frantic, silent fear as she struggled helplessly in the grasp of those two brutal men. I remembered that policeman in the shadows, and I suddenly thought: 'In spite of what that Turkish officer said, the big grafter had bribed one of his men.'

'They took me to a big house on the outskirts of Istanbul. I don't know whose house it was, but they brought my clothes, and they were intending to drive me back to my father's place today, with fresh demands for money because I had become awkward. But things began to go wrong, apparently. The telephone kept ringing, and those men with me appeared to become increasingly agitated.'

I let out my breath in a deep, gratified sigh. 'I guess Joe P. Heggy was getting into their hair right then!' It was just very unfortunate for them that I had been attracted to the window overlooking that deserted alley just when I did. And then my report to the police must have caused further alarm.

The girl went on with her story. 'I heard them give panicky instructions for some girl they knew to go and take my place in the hotel in case the police came to ask awkward questions.' I nodded, but I didn't tell Marie Konti of the not unpleasant encounter I'd had with that slim, rather heavy-browed substitute.

'This morning, though, they seemed to get in a very great panic, and suddenly that lawyer-man, as you call him, came on the scene. The situation must have seemed dangerous for him to show himself as he did because it became obvious to me at once that he was the man behind this passport manipulating and the blackmail that followed. He was very rough with his tongue. He told me that whatever I suspected I couldn't pin onto him. And he told me that if I was the slightest way uncooperative he'd see that I was sent out of the country and my father's business would be smashed. Oh, I knew he wasn't making idle talk! In this country such men are very, very powerful.

'I was ordered to return to the hotel and declare that I had been there all the time and flatly contradict everything you said.' Her soft, rounded shoulders lifted in the tiniest of shrugs. Her eyes brooded upon me. 'That's my story. Now you know everything. But I was glad when you suddenly pulled me into that taxi, because right from the moment I saw you I felt you could help me if anyone could.'

I put my arms round her then. You know how it is. You get a big, brotherly feeling and you put your arms round the girl. And then you stop feeling like a brother, but you go on keeping your arms round her, at any rate if she's a wow of a girl like Marie Konti.

And she didn't object in the least. Evidently I inspired her, and she wanted inspiration badly at that moment.

So we lay in the hot sand under the declining sun for a long time, and we talked about the plight she was in, and sometimes we didn't talk at all. It was as nice an afternoon as any trouble-buster could wish.

We swam in the soft, warm water of

that sparkling sunlit sea, and while we romped in the water she seemed to forget the menace that still hung over her, and she was as merry and laughing-eyed as probably she had ever been. But I wasn't free from thought. I knew that this blackmailing situation had got out of hand . . .

When a man as big as that politician found himself involved in a risk of exposure, you can expect anything to happen . . .

I expected it . . .

They had tried to kill me; and now I knew they would try to kill both of us. I looked at that lovely young face, and I thought: 'Not on your life. Heggy likes faces like Marie's. She's going to be around for quite a while!'

So as I swam I planned, and because my job is trouble-busting I planned to bust this other piece of trouble . . .

We changed and then took a carriage back to the harbour across the island. As we lolled on the slippery, smooth-leather upholstery, with that jogging pair of horses in front of us, I brought the subject round again to our problems. I said: 'Marie, why should your blackmailing friends try to put us behind schedule on the construction job?'

I didn't believe that myself, but I threw the thought in the air to see if Marie had some oddment of information, which might tie her troubles with Gissenheim's.

She shook her head, wonderingly. 'Did they do all that damage?' she asked innocently. So evidently she didn't know of any connection between the two affairs.

I'd been thinking along those lines myself, although there is a tendency to feel that all things are related when those things are happening to yourself. I was thinking:

'It wasn't those blackmailers. Some others, quite apart from them, are on the loose, and did it.'

And anyone's guess as to their identity was as good as mine.

Still, I had got plans made to cover any further attack on the construction site. I was rather chuckling about those plans, because I thought what eye-popping there would be from Marty and Dwight and Gorby and the other boys when they saw what I had thought up.

As we neared the wharf where the old steamers tied up, the girl's fears began to return to her. She whispered: 'Couldn't we stay on this island? I — I feel safe here.'

I looked at her and thought: 'Boy, would I like to stay on this island with you!' But aloud I said: 'Nope. They'd soon find out you were here. The thing to do is, to go out and attack them. That's the only way to break up trouble — you go out deliberately to attack it.'

She asked me: 'And can you attack it?'

I nodded. I didn't tell her she was going to be the bait to bring the trouble down within attacking distance.

I wasn't being unscrupulous in making that my plan, either. I didn't want any harm to come to this girl, but I could see only one way of smashing this menace so that she was never again affected by those blackmailers.

As we paid off our driver and started to walk along the short, crowded pier, with its bustling, gay throng of young people eternally promenading in the sunshine, I thought I saw someone familiar ahead. It was just a glimpse, and then he had gone, and I thought, surely I must have made a mistake! We went aboard the ship, and as we left the firm shore of Buyukada it seemed that a cloud descended upon that girl. Her fears returned anew, and she was holding onto my arm now as if terrified to let go of it.

She said: 'I've only you to turn to now, Joe. I can't go to the police like other people.' She looked up at me, and her big, brown eyes were pathetic. 'You won't let me down, will you?'

I told her I wouldn't let her down. I told her at length, and in detail, and the way I spoke brought the blush to her cheeks, and though her eyes dropped I knew she was pleased.

We were halfway across to Istanbul when I saw that form again. This time I knew I wasn't mistaken, but I didn't attempt to go forward and speak with the man. Instead I averted my head and got down in my deep chair alongside the girl so that I wouldn't be recognized. I wanted as much pleasure as I could from Marie's company, and that didn't require any third party.

When we were leaving the ship amid the noise and bustle of the Istanbul docks, I went forward and touched that man upon his shoulder. I did it gently, from behind, and I thought he was going to collapse. His head came round and there was almost an expression of terror in his face.

We looked into a big, fat, moon face, with eight-sided business-tycoon's glasses.

It was B.G.

And it was pathetic, his relief when he saw us. He said: 'My God, I thought it was someone else.' And then he became aggrieved. 'Why did you have to do that, scaring a fellow's pants off?'

We went across to a taxi together. I grinned, said: 'You're not on the run from little Lav, are you?'

He hung his head and mumbled something. It was something about always wanting to see Buyukada, but he didn't fool me. I knew then that B.G. had taken a boat to those distant islands in order to escape any further pursuit from little Miss Dunkley.

I kidded him a bit. I said: 'The heck, B.G., you didn't need to hide out during the daytime. She's safe enough in sunshine.' I shoved my face closer to his and said, grimly: 'Brother, it's after dark when it hits those dames. You wanna keep out of her way tonight!'

He was wanting to get into the taxi with Marie and myself, but I put my hand on his chest and held him off. I didn't see why the boss should travel in the same car as his employee. I'm no snob, but I don't always go for the company of bosses.

I said: 'Not on your life, brother. You pay your own fare.' And then I gave him a few orders. 'Listen, B.G., I want you to do something for me. I'm going out with Marie Konti to the construction site. In about three hours' time, but not before, I want you to get that information to Benny at the desk.'

B.G.'s fat face looked helplessly at me. He yammered;

'How shall I do that? What's it for, anyway?'

I soothed him. I said: 'Look, all you need do is use his desk phone and put a call through to someone. Pretend you're telling them where to find me — say, 'I know he went out to the construction site a while back. Sure, he had that dame with him. I reckon he's planning to stay out there the night with her.' Make out you're good and mad with me for playing around when I should be working, and don't let on you know there's anything deep afoot.'

B.G. blinked through his glasses at me. 'That bit about being good and mad with you for playing around will be easy,' he said, and it made me grin to hear the viciousness in his voice. He certainly would put that bit over well. Then he went on anxiously: 'But what trouble is afoot?'

He was so dumb he hadn't seen anything of what had happened to Marie Konti in the past few hours. I didn't explain. I patted him on the fat shoulder, took all his spare cash off him, and left him to find his own taxi.

We went out to the site just as dusk was falling — that quick dusk which comes when you're near the tropics.

Enormous lights now bathed that construction site, where the equipment was herded together for the night.

This night it wouldn't be in action, but the moment the repairs had been completed, it would mean a twenty-four hour working day in order to catch up on time lost. I got the taxi-driver to wait and, tucking Marie's arm under mine, I walked her to the mobile workshop, where men were working hard. I knew they were working hard because of the hammering and the bad language, which always follows when men are going at full strength.

Gorby saw me coming and started to be sarcastic about people who ducked out when there was work to be done. Then he saw who was hanging onto my arm, and he checked some of the rough words, which might have come from the Tuhlman lips.

I said: 'There's not many people working around tonight, Gorby.'

Gorby growled: 'There's not much work anyone can do until those spare are flown in.' He looked at his strap-watch on his oil-stained wrist, and said: 'I'm going any time now. We've done all we can. So far as I'm concerned, this place closes down in a few minutes, until tomorrow.'

He looked at me, his eyes grim in that sour puss of his, and he said: 'You take over then, Mr. Trouble-Buster.'

I nodded. I knew I was on duty from now on, and I liked it that way.

He messed around for a while and then got a paraffin rag and cleaned himself down. The other men were doing the same, and beginning to drift out to where the transports waited to take them back to Istanbul.

Then Gorby said, abruptly: 'The men are saying that there'll be trouble again. Maybe not tonight, but certainly again. They'll have another try to sabotage the equipment, and if you let them, by glory, I'll tear you apart with a mechanical grabber.'

I just said: 'I'll be around when any trouble starts.'

Gorby went at that and the others followed. I knew they were talking among themselves, and I knew what they'd be saying. The Trouble-Buster had brought a dame out with him to keep him company during the long, dark hours of vigil.

Their eyes said: 'Nice work, Joe!' But with it all was that sarcasm which implied: 'How d'you get these jobs, Heggy?'

I guessed that most of them would have swapped jobs with me as they saw us standing there together in the lighted doorway of the mobile workshop. Marie Konti looked her best any time, and those lights were as kind and revealing as morning sunshine.

Gorby got into the truck and then shouted: 'You won't want the lights on all night, will you?'

I called back: 'No, but keep the generator running. Maybe there'll be need for those lights at a minute's notice.'

So Gorby stuck his head out and shouted something and one of the Turkish night-guards who had been so ineffective the previous night went over to the throbbing generator to throw a switch and put us all in darkness. He didn't do it immediately but stood there, watching, until the big transport lurched and ground away across the uneven terrain.

Then he turned to look across at me, waiting to see what I wanted. I wasn't going to move until those lights were out. So I shouted: 'Douse 'em!'

He threw the switch and immediately there was a profound darkness. The moment that darkness was upon us I grabbed Marie round her slim, warm waist and trundled her off round the back of the mobile workshop. I'd got it all figured out. Behind us was the giant grab, the only equipment, according to Gorby, which hadn't been damaged. I walked with my hand outstretched, until I ran against the big caterpillar tread.

Then I fumbled around until I came up behind and found the steep steel ladder which led up to the cabin where the operator sat high above his work. I looked round into the intense darkness then but the other guards had all been clustered together around the generator, and I

216

didn't think anyone could see where I proposed to hide bonny Marie Konti.

I whispered: 'You've got to do some climbing, baby.' And I put her hand on the step rung.

She was game for anything, and at once began to ascend the steel ladder. I came up right behind, so that in fact I was almost on a level with her all the way up. I didn't want to risk a sudden attack of nerves, because we were going quite a height, and if she had fallen she would have done herself a lot of harm.

We came out on the tiny platform at the head of the steps and I held onto her like grim death in case she took a fatal step off that square-yard of steel plating.

I had the keys, and I soon found the one for the grab, and inserted it in the lock after much fumbling and got the door open. We went inside. I closed the door on us and felt safe then. Now she couldn't take a tumble and break her neck. I got into the padded seat alongside the huge levers that operated the crane. It was a nice comfortable seat, designed to keep a man happy during long hours perched high above the earth while that great grab dived and bit up tons of earth and carried it round and discharged it elsewhere. There was only one place Marie could sit, now that I was in the operator's seat.

That was on my lap.

In that darkness I reached out and my hands fell on her soft, warm young body, and I pulled her gently onto my knee. She didn't object. So we sat there for a long time, and when I kissed her she didn't object. Rather she became . . . impulsive. She was warm-blooded, and gave back all that she received.

She whispered: 'I like you, Joe. You make me feel so — safe.'

I didn't tell Marie how she made me feel. Instead I showed her.

That wasn't on the schedule, incidentally. I'd intended to park her there, lock her in, and then go off on the next part of the plan. But don't tell me any man of my age could pass up a chance like that. That wouldn't have been human, and Joe P. Heggy is always human.

But there came a time when I had to

say to her: 'The clock's going round, Marie. I'm expecting friends of yours shortly, and I've got to get ready to receive them.' She clung to me in the darkness, terrified, but I reassured her. 'Who would think of looking up here for you, sweetheart? You're all right. Just curl up in this chair and go to sleep and leave Uncle Joe to fix this party so that you'll never have any trouble again.'

I kissed her — kissed her a couple of times more because there wasn't anything nicer I could think of right then — and then I locked her in and went carefully down that ladder. I walked across and found the night-watchmen, and they had already got themselves comfortably down for a night's sleep. It's what you expect of watchmen anywhere in the world. I didn't say anything, because they weren't any part of my plans, anyway.

Then I started the long walk across to the track where the taxi waited for me with sidelights glowing. I got into the taxi and we drove away and went through the town and down to the bridge and across into the low quarter again. Then I told that taxi driver to get two or three more taxis and wait for me, because I was going to need them.

I went down an alley that was familiar to me, and then I found that broken wall, which gave down onto the wharf of that chemical factory. It wasn't pleasant, because so early there was little moon, and the way was uneven and not too familiar to me. I'd just started to go under the wharf, when I froze rigid. There had been a movement along the alley behind me.

When I stopped, that movement stopped, too.

I waited a long time, but whoever was back there didn't show, so I took a risk and began to follow that almost unseen path along the broken back wall, which supported the wharf overhead. It was a place full of shadows, with the only light reflecting from the waters fifty yards away at the end of the wharf. I didn't like those shadows, because I could think of enormous brutes of men standing there and waiting to get me as I passed. Normally I'm a giant among men, but I knew now I was in a foreign country, and these local inhabitants could make me look as weak as a child. I was among specialists in strength.

Not on your life I was!

When I found my way to that rocky little room with its sacking cover I saw the remains of a dull glowing fire there, and no one else. The boys were out again.

That did it! I'd wanted to get those boys and be away with them within minutes. But now they were essential to my plans, and I had to wait for their return. I only hoped to God they wouldn't be long!

I kicked up the fire, more to give light than because any warmth was needed that night.

And then I looked up to where that sacking curtain hung, and I saw that it was pulling gently apart.

Someone was on the other side and was taking a peek at me.

11

Nylons!

It's the Heggy way to go bald-headed. I didn't give a damn' if I was up against men of formidable strength; all I knew was that attack was probably no worse than waiting to be attacked.

I lunged forward, snarling nasty words, partly to keep my spirit up and partly to intimidate. My hands grabbed through that crack in the curtain and fell upon a body.

And I knew as soon as my fingers dug in that I'd been mistaken.

This was no man, spying on me.

I pulled, and a woman came through the curtain.

She was that young woman, the smaller of the two, who had brought my clothes back that morning. I released her, and she rubbed herself where my fingers had perhaps hurt a little.

I said: 'Sorry, sweetheart. But I didn't know I had a lady calling on me.'

She got over her scare quickly, and then she smiled at me. It was a smile that she wouldn't have given me if there had been another Turk there, especially another Turkish female. Because the Turks don't like their womenfolk smiling kindly at foreigners.

She stood there, a sturdy figure in her simple cotton garment, her mighty legs — because like her menfolk she was of massive, muscular build — her feet bare, as were her arms up to the elbows. Her big brown happy face looked at me and I knew what it felt like to be Errol Flynn in the presence of a bobbysoxer. I was as big as all that and as attractive to this Turkish maiden.

She started to move towards me, and I got scary. I thought: 'My God, if the men come back and find me with one of their gals they'll think the worst!' For certain then they'd do things to me that I wouldn't like, and they'd affect my night's plans.

The girl, though, was eager and

persistent, and she got me up against the back wall where I couldn't retreat. And there was something irresistible seeming to drive her now, to pursue me. I thought it was me, and then suddenly she spoke a word of an international language and I knew I was mistaken.

Her smile widened, and I saw big, very nice white teeth flash as she said: 'Nylons?'

It was the same old story! Go where you like in the world and everywhere you get the same question put to you if you're American — 'Nylons?' I looked at this girl, and I thought: 'You've probably never had a pair of stockings in your life, except the hideous cotton ones all the Turkish women wear in winter.'

And then I thought: 'Sister, I'm going to fill your arms right full of nylons. I'm going to make one dame happy!'

Because I remembered I had never paid her for the laundry work she and her friend had done. I nodded, and said: 'Baby, you'll get your nylons.'

Those big, brown peasant eyes looked incredulous. 'Nylons?' she repeated.

I was suddenly filled with recklessness. At times Joseph gets to showing off, and this time was one when Joe P. H. could act the big guy and it would not set him back much. At a dollar a time, stockings didn't rate high in the Heggy vocabulary; anyway, it would go on to the expenses sheet.

I waved grandly. 'Yeah, nylons.' I held up two fingers and said: 'One pair.' I don't know whether she got it, whether she understood those fingers to represent one pair of stockings or two pairs, but it didn't matter a damn. Then I flicked up two more fingers and drawled: 'Two pairs for you, honey!'

Her eyes went wider. Her mouth opened and I heard the incredulous gasp of delight as my words registered in her nylon-starved brain.

I flicked up three fingers on each hand and chanted: 'Three pairs!' I was making a fool of myself, and didn't know it. I flicked up the other fingers. 'Five pairs!' I crowed. 'Honey, I'll be down with them tomorrow — if I live!'

It was too much for her, the thought of

such joys becoming her own. She made crooning noises of ecstasy and padded forward a couple of steps on her bare feet. She held out her arms to me, and her eyes were shining. She was looking at Joe P. Heggy through a nylon veil right then, and Joe P. Heggy looked the kind of guy she'd dreamed of.

I looked at that curtain, showing in the red firelight, and I found myself licking my lips. At any moment Primitive Man might return.

I went back, away from the glowing fire, and I tried to explain things to her, but we didn't speak the same language. She'd probably never met a man who wanted to say no before in her life.

Come to think of it, I'd known only one. B.G. But he was no man. He was the boss.

She was jabbering away all the time, in a flood of language that didn't mean anything to me except l'amour.

And me with my eyes on that damned sacking curtain, and scared yellow it was going to part and a trog shove his ugly mug in.

She got herself worked up. She wanted to show her gratitude, and she wanted to be embraced and kissed by me, and she suddenly started to use her strength to get her desired ends.

Her strength . . . My God, that gal was as strong as her menfolk! She wrapped me up and lifted me off my feet, and I could feel the play of her mighty muscles under that thin — awfully thin — dress at that moment.

Just then we heard a sound . . . several sounds. That gal went spinning away from me as if I was red hot. When that curtain parted, one-tenth of a second later, she was five yards away from me, in the far corner of this rocky cell.

I looked on faces peering at me in the firelight through an opening in that sacking — hairy faces, with eyes suspicious and animal with those red lights reflecting in them. I took a deep breath and adjusted a tie that had gone round my right ear, and I said: 'Boys, you came just in time. You saved me from a fate worse than death.'

Then I looked across at that great,

strong, broad-hewn Turkish girl, and I thought: 'Oh, death, where is thy sting!' Some fate. Some gal. Some other day, I was promising . . .

And she was looking so demure that none of her menfolk suspected anything.

They came in. They didn't recognize me until I spoke, because last time we'd met I'd had my mud pack on. But their faces became almost human when they got my drawl. They'd probably had a hellofa bender on my dough and I was a fond memory to them.

I was also, right now, talking a language they knew. I had a fistful of kurus extended towards them.

I said: 'Tonight you've got to earn them. Brothers, I want to recruit you as my strong-arm boys, my muscle-men, get me?' They didn't, but I knew they'd go where all that jack went. These were the boys who would defend the Gissenheim project against all comers — and they'd take the tonsils out of the lawyer-man's apes!

I started to go out and jerked my head for them to follow. They got my meaning, but all the same they hesitated, like men saying: 'The hell, haven't we done enough for one day?' I looked at them and thought they were more than usually tired-looking and dirty, and wondered what job had kept the bunch out so late.

I tried to reassure them. 'You don't need to worry about work. There won't be any. Just now and then I'll tell you and you'll up and kill someone, that's all. It won't be like work at all, and the pay's good.'

They didn't understand a damned word, but they got my meaning. They grinned and nodded and started after me. I took one last glance at the girl, and her eyes were shining, as they looked at me. I gave her a wink. She knew then one way or another, I'd get the nylons out to her.

I stumbled along a path that was barely discernible, though the moon was stronger now. One of the porters thought he'd be kind and he picked me up and carried me right out to the end of the alleyway — and I top two hundred pounds weight.

It made me feel a cissy, but you don't argue with those boys. So I tried to look nonchalant and fished out a Camel and stuck it in my mouth and lit up. I saw grinning teeth in the moonlight and stuck a Camel between them and we both came out happily smoking.

My cab driver had two chums with him. I put the porters into two of the cars — the usual big, American sedan-type they always use out here. The drivers danced around frantically when they saw what was going in on their upholstery, and the porters hung back, overawed by those splendid vehicles. But I was down on my feet now and rapping out orders.

I shoved 'em in and bustled the Turkish drivers back into their seats. They saw my roll, and after that there was no argument. I told my driver to take me to the new airfield, and he went twice as fast as usual in an effort to please me, and I felt glad, because I had a feeling I was running against time.

Three hours had passed since B.G. had left me. If he'd wisened up Benny to Marie's whereabouts, those apes might be at the field right now looking for her. I also thought: 'Maybe the rubes who bust up Gorby's equipment might also be out there ahead of me.' And I had a happy picture of the apes and the rubes running into each other and knocking the hell out of each other. But things like that never happened in real life . . .

I knew there was something wrong when we came over the hill and I saw the brilliant floodlights on, all around the big excavation-site. The lights wouldn't have gone on unless there had been trouble.

I got the driver to go as close as he could to where that hill was sliced in half, and then I leapt out and went running crazily towards the equipment park where the machinery was grouped. I was staring at the giant grab, desperate to catch any reassuring glimpse of the girl I had left up there those few hours before, but the cabin was higher than the floods and was lost in shadow. Anything might be happening up there.

I went stumbling around the mighty equipment and vehicles, shouting as I went. There should have been plenty of watchmen around, but I couldn't see any. Then I caught a movement under the

shallow flooring of the throbbing generator, and I stooped and yanked, and a
squealing old man came into the light.

When he saw me, he stopped squealing
and tried not to look ashamed. But he
also looked into the darkness beyond
range of the lights, and he was a haunted
man. He had spent another night of
terror, and he was nearly through with
this job. When a watchman couldn't
sleep, it was time he packed up and went.

I shook him and rapped: 'What's been
happening here?' Because I could see that
things had been happening.

I could see that the rubes had been
down and torn the place apart again.
They'd given an encore before they were
expected!

As I looked at the chaos — at the
trucks with their bonnets up and their
engines mussed up, at the conveyors
lolling drunkenly over again . . . and other
confusion and damage — I heard that
excited old man's voice.

They had come right after darkness.
The other watchmen had fled, but he had
fought to his last gasp, he assured me.

They had wrecked the place and departed.

But who were they? The old man's English wasn't that good and I couldn't understand. But I was relieved.

They wouldn't have found lovely Marie Konti up in the heavens . . .

Or would they?

I started to run towards the giant grab, and then I found that old man's clinging hand holding onto me.

I stopped, turning and trying to shake him off, and saying: 'What in hell?'

Then I saw that he was haunted. Right then he was looking at ghosts. And I've never seen terror like that on his face right at that moment.

I whirled. Snarling men were almost breathing on my neck. Mighty hands were reaching for me, and the intention was to tear me apart, bone from bone, and muscle from those self-same bones.

I shouted: 'Are you crazy? I pay you — I'm the boss!' And I knew then how B.G. must have felt at times.

I shouted: 'Leave me alone!' But they didn't, and I was swept off my feet like a child, while they snarled round me like rage-maddened gorillas. Eight of them.

And I couldn't understand it. For they were the men I had brought out with me, the trogs — the porters — my muscle-men!

They started to take me to pieces.

12

Conclusion

You know, truth comes to you at the most unexpected moments. That's how it was then. Or maybe it was the inspiration which death is supposed to bring to its victims.

For in that second I was able to see my folly. I was able to understand what monumental stupidity I was responsible for.

My muscle-men were the rubes.

That's where the trogs had been, these last couple of nights. They'd been to the site, wrecking this machinery, which was a threat to their livelihood. Get machines to do a man's work, and what happens to the man? That's a question that has occupied the minds of men in every country in the world ever since the beginnings of civilisation.

And I had brought them back to the

scene of their vandalism! Oh, innocent Joseph Phineas Heggy!

But I hadn't time to indulge in mental woe. Other things were pressing. A bit more of that pressure, in fact, and J.P.H. would have been represented by a long tube of boneless pulp.

I got out of their grip. I thought up a bit of yogi, and got one trog howling and dancing, and then I threw another and beat it round the generator. They were after me, howling, their heads off, and I didn't stand a chance in the long run, and they knew it. They must have thought I'd got them to the scene of their crimes to punish them, and they weren't having any.

I jumped onto the throbbing generator footboard and grabbed for the string lamp. I tore madly at the lamp-holder, and it came off in my hands. The rubes were bounding, bare-footed, towards me, and there wasn't anything I couldn't see of them because of those bright floodlights.

I saw murder in their eyes, anyway.

'Just now and then I'll tell you and

you'll up and kill someone. It won't feel like work at all.'

That's what I had told them. And it wouldn't feel like work to these boys, in their present mood of indignation. Only, I hadn't figured on being the first corpse.

Right at the last second I thumbed apart those bare wire ends and then threw a switch. When a raging, bellowing cubic yard of muscle bounced onto the generator I just poked out and touched him on the chest.

He went back in a somersault that cleared the ground by a good five feet, and ended on his backside against a fuel hut. He sat up and looked at me, dazed, and then he started to rub his chest, and his manner said: 'Boy, do you pack a kick in that hand of yours!'

I jabbed another rube who hadn't drawn any moral from that first incident. He went back howling and cartwheeling. Then all the other trogs halted and stared at me, and they reminded me of cows standing with lowered looks.

Maybe they couldn't see those ends of wires just protruding from my fist, and they really thought I was packing a power-grab type of punch. And they respected accordingly, for they had never seen a man hit another of their kind so hard that he could knock them for a home-run in that fashion.

After a bit of hesitation, another trog did come at me, but he defeated himself by being half-hearted. He swiped to knock off the Heggy head, but I ducked and kicked and that was good enough, For he collapsed, nursing his stomach. That didn't matter much to him, and he never bore me any malice afterwards.

Then I looked down and saw the legs of that Turkish watchman. He'd gone to ground again under the generator. I tickled him with the bare ends of those wires and he came out so fast he could have broken several world records, and he was an old man.

I grabbed him and held him until he had stopped howling. I wanted that Turk because he could speak two languages. The trogs were closing in again but cautiously now, with suspicion written on their tough faces.

I shouted above the din of that throbbing generator. 'You tell these guys they don't have to worry about what they've done. Tell 'em they're on the payroll, and there's no work they have to do to earn it. Here, hand this jack out.'

I shoved a wad into the watchman's hands. Putting eight trogs on to the payroll instead of having them bust up the joint was good tactics, and Gissenheim's wouldn't bother about the expense.

That watchman's scrub face parted and he began to give out in inspired manner. The trogs were suspicious, and for a time wouldn't take the money, They didn't get things easily in their lives, I guess, and they couldn't believe what they were hearing. So I tried again.

'Tell 'em it doesn't matter a damn about what they did — just so long as they don't go on bustin' the joint. Tell 'em they can lie around and eat well and do no work for a month or two, just so long as they clump people to the ground who have no right on this land.'

They began to believe, then. They relaxed and grinned in happy delight.

Brother, had the millennium arrived! Or don't Turks have a millennium?

Carthorses of men came up and tried to demonstrate their forgiving nature. They took the dough and patted me wherever a man can be patted, and I felt like a movie god with fans again. Even the guy whose belly had been kicked came and grinned at me and held my hand for so long I got embarrassed.

I told the watchman to get food for them, but first I gave the boys their instructions. I was expecting trouble. Probably a quartet of apes would arrive, and would they please do such things to them that in the end they could only just manage to crawl — and that painfully?

Would they! I didn't get a word of what they jabbered, but I knew it added up to one thing — they were promising to take apart anyone whose mug I didn't like. When those apes arrived, they were saying what ghastly things would happen to 'em.

I started to go off towards the mobile workshop — towards the mighty power-grab, which reared up behind it. I wanted to climb up to where Marie Konti was. Back of my mind was the thought that there could be a pleasant time for me — for both of us — up there beyond the range of lights. It made my stride quicken. Marie Konti was worth hurrying for . . . and she lifted me . . . a lot.

I looked back when I was turning the end of the workshop, and at once my friends the trogs smiled and shook their heads and even laughed to show what jolly people they were, and how friendly they all felt towards me now.

I started to turn towards Marie in her sky hideout.

I was thinking: 'Let 'em all come now.' In fact I was wanting them to come, that lawyer-man and his apes.

I'd got allies now, and I felt these trogs would follow me to the death. Anyway, they'd make potato shavings of a mere quartet of apes. Yeah, boy, let 'em come and see what we'd do to 'em, I was thinking grimly, smacking my fists together at the thought.

So they did come. Immediately.

In fact they were right there at that

moment. They grabbed me as I came round the end of the workshop, just out of sight of my muscle-men. They might have been there a long time, watching — they must have come trekking across the dark wastes from a car, which had approached without headlights, and I'd run slap into their arms.

They started to give me a work-over. It was painful. One held me while the others stood around and tried to chop me down. I got the taste of blood in my mouth from the start, and I began to feel again the awful pain of those earlier beatings, for my bruises were still all there. They came in, and now they started to growl as they got worked up to their mayhem and I began to get that roaring in my ears that comes when consciousness is being slapped out of you.

It was all or bust. I just picked my feet up off the ground. That was all. But I weigh two hundred, and these apes, for all their strength, weren't trogs. I was too big a baby to hold, and that ape back of me grunted and let go of me.

I hit the floor and had sense to start

rolling. I also started to shout. I came into view of the generator and my muscle-men just as I was lurching to my feet.

The apes came at me in a succession of dives, trying to floor me before I could get moving. I thought up all the football strategy I knew to escape their tackles. I sidestepped, jumped, and found a swerve that had been forgotten for years.

They crashed into each other, and I battered off the only ape to get a grip on me. Then I found myself free and I went streaking for the generator. I started to shout to my trogs, and pointed back towards the apes. The trogs spat on their hands and looked delighted to oblige. They started to come padding forward on their mighty feet, and I stopped running to let them join me. I felt safe now. My muscle-men were a match for anyone, and they were two to one against the apes.

When they came up I turned and started to run with them, because I felt primitive then and I wanted to do a few things to those apes who had tried to chop me down.

The apes were looking worried. Some were still down on their knees. The one I'd smacked over was rolling on his back, trying to get over the agony of a badly-treated face. It looked like peanuts to the cheerleader that I was on the winning side.

And yet I wasn't.

That sleek huckster came striding into the light, suddenly. He was the personification of authority — you know what I mean . . . some men ooze power, and this lawyer-man was of the old aristocratic order who have such belief in themselves that it cannot be denied by lesser men.

Now he just waved his arms and shouted angrily, brusquely, in the direction of the charging trogs. He had guts, that boy, and he walked out quickly towards them, shouting rapidly all the time in Turkish.

You know the effect on those trogs was miraculous.

They had the strength to take that lawyer-man and his apes apart, if they had wanted to, but just his personality stopped them and made them as helpless as — carthorses. He was of the pasha class, and when pashas gave orders, a lifetime of training said they had to be obeyed implicitly.

All in one second I realized that the tables had been turned again. My muscle-men weren't a damn' bit of use to me!

That brought the apes into the picture once more. They came lurching towards me, and, holy-moly, what those babes weren't going to do to me!

I started to sprint for it. I was on my own again. The trogs just stood and looked on and would have stood and looked on no matter what I offered and what I'd given them, so far.

The apes came bounding in my rear. We streaked between the rows of trucks and bulldozers and then the car started to chase me, too. It had been standing quietly against the cliff-like side of that hill into which we had been digging. Now, when I came into view, the driver started up the engine and came roaring to cut me off . . . and run me down. It was just like old times.

I might have outdistanced the apes in a straight run in the open, but I couldn't lick that car. And dodging among the vehicles wouldn't get me anywhere with the apes on my tail. Goddamn those trogs, I swore! They'd let me down badly.

That made me think of Marie, up there in the power-grab cabin. I thought: 'If I could get up there, maybe they wouldn't think of coming up to find me.' Maybe. But I couldn't see any other way of dodging these monkeys.

I was almost through, anyway. I made one last desperate attempt — I went into the open and played suicide with that car. It missed me, and I ran on. For a few seconds I was out of sight of the apes. I went like lightning for the power grab and started to climb.

I was at the top of the ladder, looking down onto the floodlit vehicle park below. I saw the car skidding round, the apes running among the vehicles. I thought: 'I've done it. They didn't see me!'

And then that damned night watchman came running across to say a piece to the lawyer-man. That watchman figured I was a done man, and aimed to be on the winning side. He would get unpleasant things done to him when Joe P. Heggy returned to circulation!

If . . .

The apes started to come across towards the grab. I went in quickly. Marie sobbed when she saw me, and flung herself into my arms and started to kiss me. I said: 'Some other time, honey!' and stabbed for a familiar starter button. The diesels roared into life.

I could see down onto the apes now as I slid over a long lever. They had halted, uncertain. Now the lawyer-man shouted from the background and urged them to get up that ladder after me.

But I was thinking. I got the caterpillars turning, and we lurched forward ponderously. The apes came running up behind, catching us easily. I let the grab go biting down into the soft soil, and then started to swing, pulling it up — and with it, five tons of soil and rock between those steel jaws.

The apes saw what was coming and started to run for it. That big crane-boom could swing like lightning. It started to chase the apes, and I was cheering like a crazy man, up there in the box. Marie was thrilled and excited now, too.

The apes were trying to get away, and that mighty steel grab was manoeuvring overhead. They almost ran into each other, in their frantic efforts to escape, and I let the jaws open and five tons of earth came crashing down.

It didn't make a direct hit, but it sent them sprawling, and it filled them with terror. I swung round and bit off another lump of hill. I could see the lawyer-man in the background. He seemed to be urging his men to get across to that ladder while I was still loading up with dirt. They weren't moving. That mighty grab had put the fear of death into their souls. I chased them again — all of them, this time. They split up, but I kept swinging from one to the other, and that closed them again. I felt like a sheepdog, herding flock.

The lawyer-man was running now, and I liked the sight. I even took time off to point it out to Marie. He must have decided now that things were desperate enough to use a gun, even in the presence of witnesses. The windows smashed all around us, and I dragged Marie down.

I let the grab swing, and sent the muck swooshing out after the five desperately running men. It buried a couple, though they staggered out almost immediately and went streaking after their boss.

It was then that they all called it a day. Being chased by a mighty, steel mountain-shifter was something they couldn't cope with. They must have been telling the boss so, too.

All at once they headed for the car. I went after the car with an empty grab. That really must have terrified them. They piled in, and the car went swinging away instantly . . . and it crashed into the rear of the workshop. That driver must have had one desperate eye on those long, steel teeth, swooping towards them from the sky.

Those steel teeth bit around that big sedan. Screams of fear came up to us, high above the noise of diesels in the cabin. They were trapped; the doors wouldn't open against that grab.

I pulled back on a lever and threw two across. The grab went swinging skywards. The car went up with it, and we could hear the crushing of metal as the sides collapsed a little under the strain. When they were a hundred and twenty feet up, I switched off. They could spend the night there.

We went down. Five minutes later someone fell out of the grab and broke his neck. It was the lawyer-man.

We'd heard shouts from that swinging car in the jaws of the grab, and had guessed that the boys were quarrelling. No doubt the terror of their position was sending them a bit crazy. The apes argued afterwards that the lawyer-man tried to climb out of the car and fell and broke his neck. It wasn't much of a story, and our guess was they'd lost their temper and slung the boss out, but it couldn't be proved and the affair was hushed up.

That young Turkish officer didn't seem bothered by the death, either. Evidently the lawyer-man was a bit of a nuisance to the police. And with his death went this trouble prepared for Marie.

★ ★ ★

B.G. said, truculently: 'You can quit arguing, Joe. Gissenheim's are meeting trouble out at Athens, We're flying there on the noon plane. The hell with it, you've had long enough with that dame to satisfy any man . . .'

He didn't know a thing, that B.G., not about Marie anyway. I didn't want to go and leave her, even though she too had to return to Ankara soon. But . . . this was my job.

When we were circling the Corinth Canal, B.G. turned his fat face towards me and jeered: 'That's one time I was too cute for you, Joe Heggy.'

'Meaning?'

'It was a gag, what I said about trouble in Greece.' He felt so good, because he had outsmarted Joe P., that he grew fatly truculent. 'I'd had enough of Istanbul and didn't want any arguments. For land's sake, that Dunkley woman nearly got me more than once. Joe, you don't know what a time I had, trying to keep away from her.'

I said: 'You swab!' because that's a good way to address the boss. And I was filled with fury, because Marie Konti had begun to mean something in Joe P. Heggy's life. And then I snarled to myself: 'Brother, there's going to be trouble in Athens — for you!'

And there was.

I sent a cable to the Dunkley dame, giving our Athens address.

And I signed it: 'Berny Gissenheim.'

THE END

We do hope that you have enjoyed reading this large print book.

Did you know that all of our titles are available for purchase?

We publish a wide range of high quality large print books including:
Romances, Mysteries, Classics
General Fiction
Non Fiction and Westerns

Special interest titles available in large print are:
The Little Oxford Dictionary
Music Book, Song Book
Hymn Book, Service Book

Also available from us courtesy of Oxford University Press:
Young Readers' Dictionary
(large print edition)
Young Readers' Thesaurus
(large print edition)

For further information or a free brochure, please contact us at:
Ulverscroft Large Print Books Ltd.,
The Green, Bradgate Road, Anstey,
Leicester, LE7 7FU, England.
Tel: (00 44) 0116 236 4325
Fax: (00 44) 0116 234 0205

Other titles in the
Linford Mystery Library:

THE GLASS PAINTING

V. J. Banis

An old forgotten masterpiece, a painting on glass, found beneath the ruins of an ancient French mansion, had belonged to the Marquis de Garac. When Emily Hastings' sister Irene inherits the painting, they are informed that it should be given a place of honour. Soon afterwards Irene becomes mysteriously ill and signs of imminent danger point towards Emily. A strange black cat haunts the house, and then the image on the glass painting begins to change . . .

SCHOOL FOR SCANDAL

Geraldine Ryan

Three stories: In *School for Scandal*, Lucy Lockley, the Bugle's chief chief reporter, suspects the local school headmaster of being on the fiddle — then discovers something far more scandalous. Meanwhile, in *Making a Difference*, new Police Community Support Officer Shelley Lansdown normally deals with missing items — but finds herself investigating the disappearance of a family. And in *Closing Time*, DC Myra McAllister attempts to unravel a murder committed in 1962 — and appears to step back in time . . .

NOOSE FOR A LADY

Gerald Verner

Sent to trial for the murder, by poison, of her husband John, Margaret Hallam is convicted and sentenced to death. Her appeal is dismissed and the Home Secretary refuses a reprieve. Simon Gale, an old friend of Margaret, returns from painting in Italy and learns about her case. Whilst refusing to believe she's guilty, the only way he can save her is to discover the real murderer's identity. But there are no concrete clues and time is against him . . .

THE MOSAIC MURDER

Lonni Lees

The artists' reception at the Mosaic Gallery in Tucson, Arizona is a success. However, next day, the body of Armando, the owner's husband, is discovered. Every artist is a suspect, with his or her own reasons to want him out of the picture. And who stole the sculpture of the goddess Gaia? Detective Maggie Reardon investigates, but with her disastrous personal life and being viciously attacked in her home, can she survive long enough to find the culprit . . . ?

VICTORIAN VILLAINY

Michael Kurland

Professor James Moriarty stands alone as the particular nemesis of Sherlock Holmes. But just how evil was he? Here are four ingenious stories, all exploring an alternate possibility: that Moriarty wasn't really a villain at all. But why, then, did Holmes describe Moriarty as 'the greatest schemer of all time', and 'the Napoleon of crime'? Holmes could never *catch* Moriarty in any of his imagined schemes — which only reinforced his conviction that the professor was, indeed, an evil genius . . .